Fast cure for a headache . . . death!

Bolan gave his prisoner a moment to allow his mind to settle before he spoke. "The name is Bolan." He dropped a death medal on the guy's heaving chest. "That's your ticket out," Bolan continued, "and I'm hanging it on you. Get your breath, Sorenson, cause in about five seconds I'm going to route a bullet from one of your ears to the other."

The prisoner reached instant panic as the significance of the moment penetrated. "Please! Listen! I'm innocent—not one of *them!* I'm not . . . a thug!"

"Let's understand it," Bolan said, his voice cold and flat. "You're bought and paid for, a slab of meat in Morello's freezer. You make me happy and you'll live awhile. But understand—I'm not Tony Morello. I get no kicks from this. I have nothing to prove. I don't need evidence and I don't honor the fifth amendment. As you lay there now, you're a dead man. Only you can change that. Now start talking."

"I—it's—wait now—I'm just trying to make it clear!" The man's eyes were rolling, seeking. He groaned loudly and put both hands to his head. "God I think something's broken inside my head."

"You have one second, buddy, before I give you a nine millimeter aspirin. Shall we begin . . . ?"

The Executioner Series:

the EXECUTIONER
CLEVELAND PIPELINE

by Don Pendleton

PINNACLE BOOKS   LOS ANGELES

EXECUTIONER #30: CLEVELAND PIPELINE

Copyright © 1977 by Don Pendleton

All rights reserved, including the right to reproduce this book or portions thereof in any form.

An original Pinnacle Books edition, published for the first time anywhere.

ISBN: 0-523-40-150-7

First printing, October 1977

Cover illustration by Gil Cohen

Printed in the United States of America

PINNACLE BOOKS, INC.
One Century Plaza
2029 Century Park East
Los Angeles, California 90067

For *Sunny Schubert,*
a good journalist who may find reflecting fragments herein. Write on.

dp

"*How dreadful knowledge of the truth can be When there's no help in truth!*"
—Sophocles, *Edipus Rex*

"*Often there is no comfort in truth. But then I am not here to find comfort. And the final Truth is Death.*"
—Mack Bolan

Contents

CLEVELAND PIPELINE

Prologue

Mack Bolan was a man who knew the meaning of "war without end." Born during a time when the entire world was at war with itself, raised in a civilization divided by a "cold war" into East and West, matriculating into early manhood under the anxious realities of global intrigue and domino-principle international adventuring, young Bolan simply climbed a stage which the world itself had set for him—and he'd decided to become a competitor, a survivor. While other young men burned draft cards and demonstrated for peace in a world obviously bent on war, Sam Bolan's eldest son turned his excellent mind to the metaphysics of violence and the survival of human ethics.

From Nietzsche he learned: "You say that a good cause will even sanctify war! I tell you, it is the good war that sanctifies every cause!"

Young Bolan was no lover of war but he under-

1

stood the ethic perhaps best stated by another philosopher closer to home, William James: "If this life be not a real fight in which something is eternally gained for the universe by success, it is no better than a game of private theatricals from which one may withdraw at will."

Bolan took no issue with those who saw their "real fight" best waged in the cause of unilateral peace, if indeed this was a matter of personal conscience and not simply an avoidance of responsibility. In young Bolan's mind, though, the issue was not war or peace; the issue was the survival of human ethics. He had not found it within his conscience to "withdraw" from the military responsibilities in Vietnam. His government was pledged to resist aggression in Southeast Asia. Mack Bolan was an instrument of his government. And he fought the "good war" in Vietnam because his sense of rightness told him that he should.

There was a deeper ethic at work, as well. Bolan was idealistic enough to believe that gentle people should be left alone to live their own lives their own way. In his understanding, truly civilized men did not intimidate or terrorize gentle folk under any guise of politics or profits. An act of military aggression was not a civilized idea; therefore it could hardly be regarded as something "eternally gained for the universe" by its success.

The meek would never inherit a savage earth.

Bolan found his personal reasons for fighting the "good war" in Vietnam. And he became a superb soldier in every sense of the word, an admirable jungle strategist and tactician who could command himself and inspire others, a natural leader who could kill without guilt and weep without shame over the senseless killings of others. He became

2

known throughout the war theater by two telling and seemingly paradoxical nicknames: *the Executioner*, because of his incredible exploits as leader of a death team; *Sergeant Mercy*, for his compassionate attentions to the innocent victims of that war over there.

Somewhere near the close of his second combat tour, the war "over there" came to an abrupt halt for young Sergeant Bolan. Word had come from another front concerning the victims of another sort of war. The sergeant was sent home to bury his own. Father Sam, mother Elsa, kid sister Cindy, kid brother Johnny—gentle folk, all, who'd desired only to live their own peaceful lives without terror or intimidation—had fallen victim to an aggression far more savage and infinitely more dangerous than anything encountered in the jungles of Southeast Asia.

And, yes, Mack Bolan found the meaning of "war without end." He found it through the eyes of young Johnny, the sole survivor of that family tragedy, and he examined it through the conceptual ethics of Friedrich Nietzsche and William James. It was not petty vengeance or crusading morality which altered the course of Mack Bolan's life, which sent him into a one-man bloody war without end.

"A man's character is his fate," said Heraclitus.

"I am not their judge," said Mack Bolan. "I am their judgment. I am their executioner."

And so began his war against the Mafia.

Jungle fighter Bolan was taking on the largest savages of all.

1
PAYDIRT

The bad ship *Christina* was centered in the range-marks, darkly silhouetted against the nighttime glow of Cleveland, queen city of Lake Erie. To the unaided eye, the old freighter was no more than a dark blob in the jumbled shadows of the outer harbor. But Bolan knew her well, thanks to tireless surveillance and the phenomenal capabilities of his own good "ship," the *Warwagon*. The glow in the viewscreen revealed a nondescript vessel at dock, boxlike warehouses squatting beside her, a dimly lit pier along which an occasional human movement could be noted. In a finer focus, Bolan could pick out details on the ship herself: a uniformed sailor on the bridge, another at the top of the gangway, several lighted portholes along the boat deck, now and then the momentary flare of a cigarette at various points about the main deck.

Yeah, he knew her well.

5

The bad *Christina* served one Bad Tony Morello, Head Cannibal of the Cleveland mob. And the evidence of Bolan's senses was telling him that Cleveland had become the new pipeline for Mafia ambitions since the Command Strike against New York.

Sure, Bad Tony had balls enough. Cleveland could well be the new pipeline, and *Christina* could certainly be part of it. Morello owned the waterfront, his *amicu* owned the Liberian fleet which operated *Christina*, and a lot of hard shit was moving through the Port of Cleveland.

But there was more here, just at the surface, than a career psychopath such as Tony Morello could ever hope to handle entirely on his own. *Big* things were rumbling through Cleveland. A summary execution of Bad Tony would solve nothing, change nothing. Bolan had to get to the Senior Savages, those "respectable" businessmen who obviously were playing the Mafia game.

So it had been a game of wait and watch. Somewhere, sooner or later, an insulation would thin or shred, someone would inevitably trip a wire—and the Executioner meant to be watching when that occurred.

Persistence, yeah, has its own reward.

It was being rewarded now, if Bolan's instincts meant anything. A shiny limousine had edged into the viewscreen, moving cautiously along the pier toward *Christina*. Bolan sharpened the focus and punched in the laser-supplemented infrared scan to zero on that limousine. It halted a few yards from the *Christina*'s gangway and two hardmen bounced onto the pier, their pedigree apparent despite the best efforts of barber and clothier.

One of the torpedoes casually scanned the scene

while his partner helped another man debark through a rear door. Bolan zoomed on that face and started the video recorder as the third man stepped into view. What was the emotion being displayed there on that cultured face? Indecision? Apprehension? Raw fear, maybe. He was a man of about sixty, immaculately groomed in semiformal evening wear.

The frightened man was peering apprehensively up the gangway to the ship and moving slowly toward it, under escort by both torpedoes. The next move was not precisely the "spark" Bolan had been awaiting but it was spark enough to dislodge him from the sidelines as passive observer. The man in the middle suddenly whirled about and made a run for it, catching the two hoods momentarily off guard and flat-footed in their reaction.

Gun metal flashed in the optics as a snarling hardman produced a revolver. The other slapped it away and sprinted off in pursuit of the fleeing figure.

Bolan was also launched, in instant reaction. He was out of the *Warwagon* and into a waiting chase car, a Jaguar sportster, before his intellect could even begin to assess the implications of that startling "spark."

The cannibals, yeah, were hard at work—but apparently an intended victim had decided to "reason" with them from outside the boiling pot. That man was running for his life.

Bolan was running, also—for that same life. The Jag hit full revolutions during the first hundred yards of the charge and did not let off until the headlamps were sweeping the warehouse area in search of the game. He found it several hundred feet downrange from the bad *Christina*, where two big ugly cannibals were dragging a struggling victim toward the intended feast—and he joined it at full throttle, sending startled torpedoes scrambling for survival with all festive thoughts abandoned.

They dropped their prisoner with instinctive alacrity, to spin away in their own chosen paths of salvation—playing Bolan's game Bolan's way. He easily avoided the fallen prisoner and sent the charging vehicle toward instant intercept of the guy on the dock side. The sleek nose of the Jag made contact with flesh and bone, crumpling it and flinging it cartwheeling into the water with an anguished scream. The other guy had spun off to the side of a warehouse and was bringing hardware to bear on his problem when the Jag stood on her nose and Bolan erupted from there with Big Thunder unleashed. The torpedo's weapon spoke first but Bolan's spoke better, the big piece roaring out 240 grains of splattering death, totally eclipsing the lighter report of the other weapon. The Jaguar was moving in reverse even before the reverberations of that sudden encounter could move the length of the pier.

The third man had not moved from where he'd fallen. He'd been roughed up a bit. A lip was split and bleeding, one eye puffed shut. But that was only the beginning of this man's problems. Apparently he was also experiencing a heart attack.

Sounds of alarmed reaction were coming from *Christina*. There was but one sane move left for Bolan. He scooped the ailing man into his arms, deposited him in the car, and got the hell out of there.

But the guy was in bad shape, struggling for breath, the open eye plainly aware of the situation

8

and flaring into the knowledge of approaching death.

Bolan knew a bit about heart resuscitation but he also knew that this man's best chance lay at the emergency hospital just a few quick blocks away.

"Don't fight yourself," he advised. "Try to be calm. You'll have medical help in a minute."

But the guy was trying to tell him something.

"Don't talk," Bolan said firmly.

The dying man insisted nevertheless, the voice weak and the tortured words all but indistinguishable. "... pro shop ... great danger ... help her ... the girl ..."

Bolan's first item of business was to get the dying man to the hospital, and he beat his estimated time by about ten seconds. The guy was still gasping the urgent message—even more urgent than his own life itself, apparently—when the Jag powered along the drive to the emergency entrance and pulled onto an ambulance ramp.

A uniformed cop was standing there.

"Cardiac!" Bolan snapped at him. "Get some help out here!"

The cop's gaze strayed to the victim's face. He paled, then quickly went inside without a word to Bolan.

The old man had stopped breathing. Bolan ran around to the passenger door and hauled the guy out, lay him on the ground, and commenced CPR. A couple of orderlies appeared a moment later and smoothly took over. Another guy with a stethoscope dangling from his neck appeared then, and continued the CPR procedure while the others lifted the patient onto a gurney.

Bolan's mind was now fixed on the necessity for a quick fadeaway, but the cop was holding the door for their entrance and his concerned comment to the attendants stayed Bolan's departure another moment.

"Take good care of the judge, boys."

Bolan froze at midstride, torn between the need to fade and the almost equally important need to know. Another moment and the cop would be wanting answers to some questions of his own.

Too late already. The cop was giving him an expectant look. Bolan fell in behind the procession and went inside.

People were gathering around, applying oxygen and doing the other usual things as the "judge" was hurried toward a treatment room.

Someone gasped, "Hell—it's Judge Daly!"

The cop was looking Bolan up and down—wondering, maybe, if and where he'd seen that face before.

The "most wanted" man in the country did not give the guy too much time to wonder about it. "Call it in!" he snapped. "Be sure someone notifies the family!"

The cop reacted immediately to that voice of quiet authority, spinning on his heel and walking quickly toward the desk.

It was cut, now; to follow through seemed the only logical action. Bolan followed through. He went into the emergency treatment room and grabbed the intern by the arm. "What's his chances?" he quietly inquired.

"How long was he gone before you instituted CPR?"

"Just a few seconds."

"That could be the determining factor," the intern said. "We'll get him stabilized and then—"

"I'm a police officer," Bolan lied. "I need to talk to him. Now."

"That's impossible," the guy replied angrily. "The man is barely alive."

Perhaps. But the man was conscious and still trying to talk. Bolan brushed past the intern and bent low to catch the labored speech. "... Mel ... girl ... plot ... help ..."

"Where is she?" Bolan asked. "Where is the girl?"

"Pro ... pro ..."

"Right, the pro shop. But where? Where is the pro shop?"

The judge muttered something that sounded like "pine group."

Bolan's eyes asked the question of the intern.

"Pine Grove, probably," the guy told him. "It's a country club on the west side. Now you've simply got to—"

"Sparks," Bolan said quietly.

"What?"

"Take care of the judge," Bolan said, and he went out of there.

The cop was still at the telephone.

Bolan waved as he went past. He reclaimed his chase car and turned her head westward.

Sparks, sure. Paydirt. A federal district judge, Mafia torpedoes, a country club, a girl in jeopardy, a plot, great danger. Paydirt for damn sure.

"Thanks, judge," Bolan whispered to a brave spirit. "I'll take it from here."

2
LOCATORS

The local chamber of commerce liked to think of Ohio's largest city as "the best location in the nation." And maybe it was . . . for many things. Within a five-hundred-mile radius was concentrated more than half of the entire population of both the U.S. and Canada, fifty-five percent of all the country's manufacturing plants, and more than fifty percent of all retail sales in both countries. One of the busiest ports in the nation, it handled traffic not only from the Great Lakes but from the world at large via the St. Lawrence Seaway to the Atlantic and from all the great industrial rivers of the continent via inland waterway to the mighty Ohio.

Only the cities of New York and Chicago could claim more corporate headquarters than Cleveland—and this proud center of America's industrial heartland did not mince words in staking its claim, pointing to the biggies like Goodyear and Firestone, Standard Oil of Ohio and Republic Steel, General Tire and TRW. Sherwin-Williams, Addressograph-Multigraph, American Shipbuilding—on and on, count them, forty-one of the top one thousand industrial corporations in the country were headquartered here.

A good location, sure.

One of those "top corporations" not mentioned in the Chamber of Commerce brochures was *La Cosa Nostra*, whose annual gross "product" exceeded that of many small nations. The Mob was not headquartered here, of course, but it maintained a thriving branch office in this industrial heartland of the nation.

And so what was "going down" in Cleveland?

What was a veteran legbreaker and contract specialist such as Bad Tony Morello finding in common with so many respected pillars of the business and social communities? Gambling, narcotics, prostitution, pornography—sure, the usual nickel-and-dime operations from which pyramiding fortunes were built—it was common knowledge that Morello was local master of all that.

But there was more, much more—and Bolan had so far picked up only the vibrations of some ambitious new trust at the innards of American industry. He had followed those vibrations to Cleveland—"the best location in the nation"—and hit a stone wall.

The developments of this evening—as small as they seemed, on the surface—were the first faint crack in that wall. Bolan had absolutely no "feel" for Judge Edwin Daly. It was nothing new or particularly startling to find a federal judge playing the cozies with a Mafia boss. It was a bit strange, however, to find one running for his life from a couple of legbreakers. All sorts of interesting possibilities were thus presenting themselves to Bolan's trained and knowing mind as he sought out one of the most exclusive country clubs in this city of corporate exclusiveness.

He followed Interstate 71 south to an exit just beyond suburban Brook Park, then maintained a due westerly course—occasionally consulting a road map on the seat beside him—until the intersection with Pine Grove Road, a two-lane blacktop bordering the sprawling country club.

The time was close to three o'clock. The grounds were dark, silent, almost forbidding as he turned into the drive and killed his lights. He sat there for a moment to get the feel and lie of that place and to allow his eyes to adjust to the darkness. Then he continued on, climbing slightly for another few hundred yards in a winding approach to the clubhouse.

The place reeked of class.

Low, modern lines with a lot of rock and glass—reflecting pools in the front, swimming and other frolicsome facilities fanning off to the side, plenty of trees and sleek lawns, hedgerows, flowers, bowers, flagstone walkways peeling off in all directions.

A couple of floods lit the front lawn. Faint nightlights glowed at the rear. There were no signs of security guards or night watchmen—indeed, no sign of human presence whatever.

Bolan pulled his vehicle into a stand of trees at the edge of the parking area and quietly got out to sniff the night. It was then he heard the murmur of distant voices. He quickly stripped down to the black combat outfit which he wore beneath the street clothes and thoughtfully selected his weapons. There was no way to anticipate what may be encountered during the probe. Perhaps nothing more threatening than a steward or janitor. On the other hand . . .

When he left the vehicle, the .44 AutoMag head-buster was riding military web at the right hip and the 9mm Beretta Brigadier—silencer equipped—rode shoulder harness beneath the left arm. Spare clips for both pistols were touch-placed at the waist. Special accessories, routine for such missions, occupied slit pockets of the blacksuit. Black sneakers on the feet completed the rig.

A light probe, yeah. Hopefully. He blended with the night for a quick and silent recon, remaining well clear of the lighted areas, carefully testing the darkness as he homed in on those muted voices.

The judge had mentioned the pro shop, which should be over toward the golf course. But there was nothing but darkness out there—and there was no need to travel beyond the main clubhouse.

Those voices were coming from the pool area. Male, two of them, a bit argumentative but seemingly allied in some joint enterprise. Some damn *deadly* enterprise, yeah.

"I say we put a bathing suit on her."

"Bullshit, go find one then."

"I could find one. They got a whole shop full of them in there."

"Forget it. This is just as good. She was here alone, see, after everybody left. She decided to have a swim. Why not bare-assed? Who's to look?"

"God it's almost a shame, ain't it? *I'd* look at *that* any day."

"Stop, you're breaking my heart. It's just another broad, Lenny. A *wise* broad, at that. Now gimme a

16

hand here, dammit. If she tries kicking me in the balls again, I'll have your ass."

"I guess she's all kicked out. Lookit that, would you? She's screaming with her eyes. She's afraid to open her mouth." The guy chuckled wickedly. "She believed you, Chuck. She really thinks you'll give her something to chew on."

"I'll give *you* something to chew on if you don't stop dicking around. Grab her feet, dammit."

Bolan had then in view now.

The submerged lights inside the pool were providing a rather mellow illumination to the macabre scene at poolside. A beautifully voluptuous and quite naked young lady lay passively on her back at the water's edge. At this point, Bolan did not have a clear view of her face but he had the impression that she was conscious and aware. Strangled little sobs on the borderline of hysteria provided a strange contrast to the docile manner in which she was accepting an unhappy fate. The two guys were standing waist deep in the pool, preparing to drag the girl in with them.

A chain-link fence stood across Bolan's way and the gate was at the far end. He hit that barrier at the run, vaulting over and landing lightly on the other side at almost the precise spot where the girl had been lying. She was now in the water, submerged between the two fully clothed torpedoes, horrified eyes open and—yeah, Lenny—*screaming*.

The two savages seemed to be getting some weird kick out of the girl's suffering. Apparently they had been playing with her for some time, holding her just barely submerged and perhaps even hauling her out at intervals—purely in the interests of game preservation—prolonging the

17

drowning and in the process reducing that fragile mind to a paralyzed lump of passive terror.

It had been awhile since Mack Bolan had felt such compassionate rage.

Those bulging blue eyes were staring up at him—and he knew that she *saw*, six inches of water and mindbusting terror notwithstanding. Bolan knew, too, that she had never lost hope, had never totally surrendered to the terror.

Lenny's eyes had caught something also—traveling up from the girl's feet and slowly lifting into that confrontation with icy outrage.

"Oh shit," he muttered.

They were appropriate last words. The big silver hawgleg thundered its disgust with savage games. A chunk of Lenny's head skipped off across the water, trailing muck and crimson fluids behind it.

The other guy turned loose of the girl as though she had suddenly developed great heat, hands rising toward the stars in a silent plea for mercy. Bolan sent the guy all the mercy he could find, a big mushrooming bullet squarely between the eyes. Then he snatched that tormented girl from the muck and delivered her from terror, carrying her tenderly to his breast and murmuring soothing words of reassurance.

He took her to a sunning board and gently lay her down, manipulating cold arms and abdomen to assist her in expelling unwanted fluids. She spluttered and coughed in cooperation but those terrorized eyes never left his until he got up and went in search of her clothing. He dressed her, slung her bag over his shoulder, then lifted her again into his arms and carried her away from that abominable place.

He'd come for answers and found only more questions.

But Mack Bolan was not complaining—and all the new questions could await a better time and place. So could the Executioner. Sparks—yeah, maybe. But it had definitely become a night for Sergeant Mercy.

And that was okay, too.

3
IDENTITIES

Bolan took the girl to his "safe house" on the West Shore and put her to bed. He was a bit concerned about her condition but—knowing the enemy—he was also reluctant to entrust her safety to others until he learned the full dimensions of her problem. He had seen too many cute kids—or what was left of them—who'd incurred the wrath of human monsters in the Mob.

But she had told him nothing whatever, and he was sort of stuck with her for the moment. The physical condition seemed okay. The breathing was a bit rapid but the pulse was good, the eyes looked okay, the body was unmarked except for a couple of small scrapes on the backside. It was her mental condition that was bothering Bolan. At first, she'd acted almost as someone in a waking trance—seemingly conscious and aware yet totally unresponsive to his presence. She'd said not a word, not even with those great eyes which had been so expressive in the knowledge of death. Those eyes closed at some point during the quiet journey. She seemed to be sleeping but Bolan could not be sure of even that.

Thanks to a driver's license found in her purse, he knew her name and vital statistics. The only other identifying items were a couple of credit cards, which told him only that she was a good credit risk. Beyond those, nothing. So he'd simply put her to bed and hoped for the best.

Bolan went to the telephone then, and began the involved procedure toward a "clean" telephone contact with his friend and confidante in the enemy camp—the one and only Leo Turrin, undercover fed extraordinaire. He direct-dialed a New York number and received a sleepy "yeah" on the third ring.

"La Mancha?" Bolan inquired.

"You got the wrong number, dammit, at four o'clock in the damn morning!" was the angry response.

Bolan said, "Go to hell, then," and hung up.

He lit a cigarette and went to the kitchen to kill a necessary five minutes before returning to direct-dial another New York number. That good voice at the other end was still a bit thick with sleep but the nature was good. "Don't you ever sleep?" it asked him.

"Some day I'm going to," Bolan soberly promised. "I think I've struck a spark here, Leo."

"What's happening?"

"I'm hoping your encyclopedic mind can tell me that. Put a federal district judge in your computer for me. The name is Daly."

"Yeah. Edwin, I think. Ohio, northern district."

"That's the one," Bolan assured him.

"Far as I know, he's clean," Turrin reported.

"Maybe that's the problem, then," Bolan mused. "Someone leaning on him?"

"I think so, yeah. I'll need some help here, Leo."

"Okay. I'll get you all his present sitting cases. What else?"

"A lady. Name is Susan Landry." Bolan spelled it. "Age twenty-three, residence Cleveland. Eyes blue, hair brown, height five-six, weight one twenty-five. Everything in the right place and plenty of it. Carries a BankAmeriCard and Master Charge. Do you need the numbers?"

"No. What's her problem?"

"Remaining alive."

"I see." The little fed sent a heavy sigh across the connection. "Do you ever meet any other kind, guy?"

"Not usually," Bolan admitted wryly. "I need her pedigree, Leo."

"I'll see what I can do. But listen. You're liable to encounter a lot of those in Bad Tony's territory. He collects them by the bushels."

"I don't read it that way with this one," Bolan said.

"Well . . . okay. But listen, that guy cleared a cool five mil' last year on his porn interests. He's got everything from vibrating dildoes to snuff films. So—"

"Give me that last again."

"You know what a snuff film is."

"I think so. But let's make sure."

"Sickies. The star always dies. I mean really dies."

Bolan sighed. "Yeah, okay. South American traffic—right?"

23

"Not exclusively," Turrin said. "Not even usually, anymore. I've heard about a couple that were made in this country."

Bolan said, "Okay, thanks. Maybe I'm closer than I thought. About, uh, that judge, Leo . . ."

"Yeah?"

"Look into his love life."

"Okay."

"You might want to do a number on the Pine Grove Country Club, too."

"That's in Cleveland?"

"Metro area, yeah. Something's out of focus there. You've heard of the Cleveland Fifty?"

"Should I?"

"Maybe not. It's a social tag, the cream of local society. Pine Grove is their club. But a couple of Bad Tony's legbreakers were making like it's their own private playground."

"Did you say *were*?"

"That's what I said, yeah."

Another strong sigh came back at Bolan. Presently the little guy told him, "Watch that guy, Sarge. He's not called *Bad* Tony for nothing. I mean, he kills for kicks. You know?"

Bolan said, "I know. How do you read him as the Boss of Bosses?"

Turrin seemed to be considering the idea. There was a long silence, then: "He's got balls enough, that's for sure. And you've given him a clear track. Yeah, sure. There's no one *here* anymore to tell him no. He never got along too well with the New York crowd. Most of his ties lead westward. Big land interests in Arizona and Nevada. But . . . yeah. If he could come up with the right deal, I think the others might go along. He could be your man."

Bolan said, "Nothing is on the surface here, Leo.

But every time I close my eyes, I see a giant octopus writhing all over this town. It's being eaten. And I can't even find the feast."

"Look for fat men, then," Turrin wryly suggested.

"Exactly what I'm doing," Bolan told him. "Okay. I'll try to hit you again sometime today. Go back to your warm bed. And tell the lady hello."

"She lights a candle for you every morning, Sarge."

"I didn't know that."

Turrin chuckled. "Any other guy in the world, I'd be jealous. There's a lot you don't know, guy. I bet there's thousands of candles burning in your name right at this very minute. Hey. I light one myself."

Bolan was genuinely touched but he kept the secret. "Stay hard, Leo," he said, and hung it up.

Candles were okay, sure. As symbols of care and concern, they said a lot. Bolan's guns were the same kind of symbols, though, and they also said a lot. They said that Mack Bolan cared. His cares were getting stronger, too, the deeper he delved into this Cleveland mess.

"Thanks for the candle, Leo," he muttered, and went to the bedroom to look in on the latest care.

It was a terrible, grotesque dream. She was sailing on Lake Erie when this horribly violent squall came from nowhere and nearly capsized the boat. The waves became monstrous, continually washing the deck and clutching at her, trying to drag her overboard. And the rain was beating down in a merciless wind-driven torrent, entering her mouth and nose and choking her. It was terribly dark and she could not even see the shore. The squall was driving her farther and farther out and she could not bring the boat around. Then suddenly this huge giant appeared, way out on the horizon, suspended above the water, towering over everything—a man, but a giant of a man—clad in a black, tight-fitting suit of some sort, belts and military things strung across his chest. The squall was driving her straight toward the giant. She was very frightened—no, she was positively horrified. The giant was holding out his arms, reaching for her across a vast distance, those arms growing longer and longer . . . uh, no . . . huh-uh. This was a friendly giant. He was going to rescue her from the storm. His eyes were all warm and concerned—but just a moment earlier they had been . . .

She sat bolt upright on the strange bed in a strange room and fought to keep the hysteria down, wishing the dream would come back. The friendly "giant" was standing there at the foot of the bed with those same worried eyes, bringing all the reality back in a crashing realization of all that had been.

"You're looking better," he said in an incredibly soft voice, then immediately left the room.

Better than what? she wondered vaguely. Her hair was stringing down around her shoulders, the blouse was ripped and dirty, her skirt was damp and wrinkled beyond hope. So what the hell had she looked like *before?*

The giant returned, carrying a small plastic tray with two plastic cups. He sat down beside her and placed the tray on her lap. "I made some hot chocolate," he said solemnly. "Let's give it a try."

Any man who offered a girl hot chocolate in bed, in the middle of the night, could not be all bad.

She sampled the offering and told him, "It's good, thanks."

He took his cup and moved to a chair. In that same solemn tone he'd used with the chocolate, he told her, "We need some words, if you're feeling up to it."

She was "feeling up to" a screaming fit, that was what, but she replied, "Sure. For openers, thanks. I don't know where you came from but God I—" She was suddenly very strongly aware of the dampened clothing and then—entirely illogically—flamingly embarrassed.

But he was a nice guy, yes. He turned away from that as he asked her, "How much do you remember?"

Very quietly she replied, "I remember you dressing me. Then I guess I passed out."

"I meant before that."

"Oh, I remember every dismal detail," she said dully.

"Stand up," he said.

"What?"

He smiled soberly. "Check out all your parts."

"I'm fine," she assured him, lying through her teeth, "just fine."

He stood up and went to the door, then turned back to tell her, "The bathroom is straight ahead. Use the terrycloth robe on the back of the door, if you'd like. Your purse is on the dresser. I'll be in the kitchen."

And he left her sitting there all damp and misty-eyed hysterical with a cup of damn chocolate in her lap.

He was not the most talkative damn giant she'd ever met! But he sure got the message across. Get yourself in hand, Susan. You must look like the Witch of the West!

Wow, damn, what a man!

She struggled off the bed and wobbled to her feet, snared the purse, and took her cup of chocolate to the bathroom. It was an apartment, pretty nicely appointed but rather neutral—highrise. She could see—hell, she was at the Gold Coast.

She stripped off the abused clothing and examined her hurts, then stepped into the shower and gave it all the heat she could take. The hair was hopeless, just hopeless. She toweled it dry and piled it high, then draped the towel around it. If you can't fix it, hide it—right? Right. The terrycloth robe was ridiculous. Susan was no small kid, but that damn thing made her feel like an underprivileged elf. She gathered it around and cinched it up as best she could.

She felt like a damn teenager!

Her heart was pitty-patting. And she could hardly wait to get that sober giant in sight again.

This was ridiculous!

She stepped into the kitchen and told him, "All my parts are here. Thanks to you. Say, you are really—I mean, you were something fine back there. And we're total strangers. I mean . . ."

Those concerned eyes were tearing her up. He said, very softly, "I know *who* you are, Susan. What I need now is *what* you are."

"That makes us even then, superman," she replied, looking him up and down. "I know *what* you are. All I need, I guess, is *who*."

He gazed at her for ever so long, no expression at all in those eyes; then he told her, "I'm Mack Bolan."

"Oh God," she said weakly.

And she wished that she was on the lake, sailing her boat in a storm.

4
ROLES

Mack Bolan's war against the Mafia had been making headlines around the world for quite a while. He'd been the subject of television news specials and he'd been endlessly analyzed and dissected in magazines, newspapers—and even a series of books were being written to chronicle his exploits. Pretty soon, no doubt, the movies would be taking off with fictional expositions of his war. He'd become something of a "legend in his own time." None of this had any direct effect upon the man himself or upon his war. He was still more ghost than reality to the majority of the world's people. Even his enemy knew him more from his effect than by any firsthand encounter. Very few living *mafiosi* could offer any valid description of the man except in the vaguest of terms. Dozens of composite sketches had been tried and circulated widely, yet none had captured a worthwhile likeness. He had resorted to plastic surgery early in the war—very successful surgery—which rendered earlier photos totally invalid. The enemy itself had committed the supreme blunder of murdering the plastic surgeon after his technical sketches had been destroyed.

Adding to the general anonymity was Bolan's expertise in what he called "role camouflage." An "adaptability" learned in the war zones, this involved the true art of physical illusion without use of gimmicks. He had the knack of simply projecting an image of innocuous identity to other minds.

"Eyes and ears are simply instruments," he once explained to a friend. "They record what is there, sure. But it's the mind that comprehends. I don't play to the eyes and ears. I play to the mind."

As is the case for all living legends, Bolan was of course a figure of considerable public controversy. Some applauded him and his effect. Some were outraged by his extralegal activities. Some were simply amused and entertained by the thought that a guy could beat the system in such a dramatic fashion. And perhaps some, as Leo Turrin suggested, lighted candles for him.

He had learned to accept the full range of response, without puffing or shrinking at any of it. He was doing what had to be done, period. People could take it however they chose.

But Mack Bolan was human. He was not totally unaffected by personal censure. He was not totally unaffected by lovely young women such as Susan Landry. And no sane man enjoys being regarded as some kind of monster.

The girl's whole manner altered abruptly the instant he introduced himself. He thought for a moment that she was going back into that trancelike state. But then those blue eyes crackled with some

30

inner fire. She whipped the towel from her head and angrily muttered, "Oh fine, that's great! And all I was worried about was my lousy hair!"

She went to the stove and banged the pan of chocolate from burner to burner, then turned to him with both hands at her head. "Do you have a hairbrush?" she inquired calmly.

He shook his head. "You look fine. Forget it. There are larger worries."

She turned the full force of those blues on him as she replied, "You bet there are. And now I've got a damn vigilante on my hands."

He said, "Funny, I thought it was the other way around."

She made an odd little gesture with both hands and told him, "Look, it's okay! You saved my life. Okay. Thanks. Now what?"

"That's up to you," he replied coldly.

"So goodbye and good luck." She stepped off firmly and moved across the kitchen. "I'll just get my things. Thanks for the use of the horse blanket."

"The town is crawling with those guys," he told her backside. "They'll find you if they want you. And I'd say they want you, lady."

She spun about in the doorway to give him a measuring look. "Why are you in Cleveland?"

"To bust it," he answered candidly.

"What makes you think there's anything to bust?"

He showed her a solemn smile. "Why were two of Morello's crazies helping a naked lady drown in the Fifty's swimming pool?"

She flushed brightly and said, "Nuts! All I owe you is thanks and I'm not even sure I owe you that. How do you know they really meant to kill me?

And you would have killed *them* whether I was there or not. Don't deny it."

He asked her, "What do you think I should have done with them?"

"Anything but that!" she spat. "That's the trouble with men like you! You have a single answer to every problem in the world, don't you? Just kill it, kill the problem with a gun. You make me *sick*."

Some things made Bolan sick, too, but it was not the poor misunderstood cannibals who occupied his sympathies. He told the "sick" young lady: "You've got your values scrambled. The issue is not justice. It's survival. And I'm not a vigilante. I'm a soldier."

"And you take no prisoners!"

Right, I take no prisoners. Haven't you heard the news? Our courts have revolving doors. Those two boys I burned tonight—have you ever seen the rap sheets on those guys? Lenny Casanova has been up for everything from raping an eleven-year-old girl to beating an eighty-year-old woman to death with her own shoe. Ten counts of assault with intent, two whole pages of intimidation for shakedown, and almost as many suspicions of murder. All that was before he graduated from the tender mercies of the juvenile court system. He hasn't even been touched since Morello took him in hand. As for Charlie Guisti—he's the one who taught Lenny all the cute tricks that made him Morello's number two legbreaker."

All of which had no visible effect on the angry young lady. I've heard all those arguments before," she snapped back. It doesn't change right and wrong. We can't sink to their level. There has to be a better way."

"I hope there is," Bolan said quietly. "And while

you and I are debating the question, your city is being eaten whole."

Anger was moderating to exasperation. "Look," she said, "I'm sorry I blew off. I can't help the way I feel. But I am not ungrateful. Let's get that understood. So what do you want me to do to prove it? What do you want from me?"

"I just want to understand," he told her.

"Understand what?"

"You."

She changed colors again, leaned against the doorjamb, fussed with the robe. Bolan was struck once again by the beauty of this woman. It was not a mere matter of planes and angles, curves and textures—though there was that, also; it was something else, something indefinable, something fine.

She said, "Look, I'm trying very hard to understand *you*. Now for God's sake, don't ask me to try understanding myself."

"Let's start with easies, then. What were you doing at the country club?"

She tossed her head, apparently still aggravated by the mussed hair. "I work there," she said. "Let's start with reciprocals. What were *you* doing there?"

"Looking for you," he told her.

"Sure."

"Truly. Judge Daly sent me."

That brought a reaction. Those seething blue eyes jerked and receded just a bit, then fell to an inspection of her toes.

"I find that . . . just a bit confusing," she said haltingly.

He said, "Reciprocals—remember?"

"Well, okay, sure. Listen, this is . . . you're never going to buy . . . I mean . . ."

33

He told her, "Morello had a couple of arms on Daly, too. I shot them away from him but the judge collapsed with a heart seizure. I took him to the hospital. He told me a girl needed help. It seemed very important—more so than his own life. He thought he was dying."

She seemed highly interested. "But he isn't?"

Bolan shrugged. "Doctors do fabulous things with heart victims these days. What sort of work are you in? At the club, I mean."

"I'm an assistant manager."

"What do you manage?"

She smiled grimly. "Everything I can."

"You weren't doing so well at the pool."

"Well, you can't win them all," she said sweetly.

"You're not going to tell me a damn thing, are you?" he decided.

"Not if I can help it, no. We're competitors, Mr. Bolan."

"We are?"

"Yep."

"You a cop?"

"Nope."

"Moll?"

"*Hell* no!"

"So what are we competing for?"

She smiled. "Let's just call it . . . an ideal."

"I hope your ideals don't kill you, Susan," he told her, and meant it.

"Which hospital did you take the judge to?"

He told her, then added: "Don't go there. Don't call and don't try to contact any of his associates. Morello will have everybody wired. You too, probably, so stay clear of any place that can be connected to you. Don't use your credit cards. Don't write any checks. Don't—"

"It sounds like I'm on the lam," she observed, eyes gleaming.

"You better believe it," he assured her. "And it's no game, so don't take it lightly."

"You're really serious, aren't you?"

"I really am."

She shivered. "Okay. It sounds like you know all the rules. I guess you must. They've worked okay for you so far, haven't they? Okay. Thanks. Now I really must go."

"No need to," he told her. "The place is yours, the rent is paid, it's safe. I won't be returning to it."

He stepped past her and headed for the exit.

She said, "Well, wait!"

"The waiting is ended," he said, from the door.

"Well, where can I contact you!"

"You can't."

"Hey! Listen! I'm sorry! I mean . . . you're a nice guy. Be careful."

Well, he'd progressed from "vigilante" to "nice guy"—but that was as far as it was going to go, that much was plain. As for the girl, whatever her role in the Cleveland pipeline, he could only hope that it did not smother her. Clearly he could not impose protection upon one who rejected it.

He smiled at her, said, "God keep," and went out of there.

And, yeah, the waiting was over.

5
SCENES

Tony Morello had been a small-minded punk all his life. He still was. At the center of the man was a nasty kid who'd never grown up. Not to say that he was not dangerous. In terms of sheer brute strength and animal cunning, Morello had few peers in the underworld. Add to that a natural ferocity and quick willingness to strike and you had the perfect picture of a Mafia bully boss. Which is exactly what the guy was. So far as Bolan could determine, the man had not a true friend in the world. Many feared him, but fear is no satisfactory basis for friendship—nor even for true leadership. It was remarkable, then, that the guy was still alive and bullying at the age of fifty.

Even more remarkable, to Bolan's turn of mind, was the fact that this sadistic bullyboy had been able to engineer so many satisfying "connections" within the straight society of a city such as Cleveland.

Morello himself was not the core of the Cleveland problem; this was Bolan's conviction. Left alone to his own devices, Bad Tony would be out hustling the streets with girls, drugs, and the usual petty scams—perhaps a contract murder here and there, a few floating crap games, oddjob muscling. But someone had lifted Tony Morello above all that—someone with clout and business acumen, someone with the vision to build and a willingness to rob. Someone "straight." Tony Morello was nothing but a muscle.

Who in Cleveland needed and wanted that muscle? Wanted and needed it enough to put up with a nasty kid who killed for kicks and tortured as a relief from boredom?

The question itself could provide a logical assumption in many localities. Not so in Cleveland. The town was too stable in its foundations to provide a ready solution. The business community was healthy. The labor picture more or less placid. The politics relatively dignified. There had been no rampant corruption in local government since the heyday of the old Mayfield Road Gang.

Cleveland had never been a real cushy Mafia stronghold. The Jewish racketeers had pretty much dominated the area in the old days. Even the Mafia *don* who initially represented Cleveland on the national *commissione* was known to be little more than a spokesman for the real—Jewish—boss of Cleveland. Reform movements begun in the thirties sent the gangs to the suburbs and then to the hinterlands of Ohio, finally pushing them across the border into Kentucky. The real power began moving west long before that—to Las Vegas, Phoenix,

Tucson, Southern California. Tony Morello was the heir to what was left behind—which had not been much, until very recently.

Now, suddenly, Cleveland was vibrating to the flow of *big* money moving along conduits below official eyelevel—a pipeline operation—and the nasty kid from Akron was seated squarely astride it. Bolan could have quickly and painlessly blown Tony Morello out of the saddle at almost any time during the past few days. He had wires all over the guy, had penetrated a dozen of the guy's front operations, and had even paid a couple of quiet visits to his headquarters—an old riverfront estate on the Cuyahoga. But Bolan wanted more than the rider; he wanted the mount, also; he needed to put a few more wires around Bad Tony's rotten neck.

It was nearly dawn and the old joint on the river was still ablaze with lights. Half a dozen cars were in the graveled parking area. Tired-looking men with shotguns cradled at the chest walked their monotonous posts. A couple of cute kids with more beauty than brains and more flesh than cover boredly sipped drinks on a lighted patio behind the house. Deep male voices raised in anger could be heard through an open window on the second floor. The cute kids kept tossing nervous glances that way, almost as though half expecting a body to come flying out at any moment.

Bolan was in blackface and blacksuit. He carried no weapon save the silent Beretta, a stiletto, and a nylon garrote. Twice in the past few minutes the garrote had bitten deeply into sentry flesh. But the "soft penetration" had reached an impasse at the patio, and the girls seemed to be planted there for the duration of whatever was going down inside the house.

Bolan began a circling movement, seeking another angle of entry. Just as he reached a point directly opposite the front entrance, the door opened and none other than Bad Tony himself stepped outside.

He was alone.

Bolan froze and watched as the bullyboss lit a cigar, then casually strolled to the parking lot.

Someone was waiting for him, in one of the vehicles.

Morello went halfway, stopped and gazed around, then casually lifted an arm. A slight man with thinning blond hair stepped out of the car and joined Morello; then the two of them took a walk along the garden path.

Bolan went with them, keeping his distance until the two halted at a cement bench and sat down. As far as Bolan could determine, neither had uttered a word since the meeting and still nothing was being said.

Morello sat and puffed the cigar.

The thin man sat quietly and nervously and looked at his hands. He was a guy of maybe thirty-five, neatly dressed, intelligent looking.

Presently Morello rasped, "So what went wrong?"

The guy squeezed his hands together as he replied, "I don't know, Tony. I just don't know. They had the girl in the pro shop when I left. I wasn't really in favor of this, you know. I didn't approve of it."

"No kiddin'."

"No, I am not kidding. This is all just crazy. Of all places to try something like—"

"Shut up!"

"I just meant—"

"I know what you just meant. Who ever asked you to approve of anything? Huh? Since when do I give a shit what you *favor* and what you don't?"

The thin man had not a word in reply to that.

"I asked you what went wrong. You give me mealy mouth. I send my two best boys out there to do a routine job for you. My two best boys are found floating in their brains. Now I'm asking you, Sorenson. What went wrong?"

"The whole thing was wrong from the beginning!" the guy wailed. "I never *dreamed* you meant to—to—to do *that*! I thought you'd pay her off or scare her off or whatever you do in these situations. Those idiots were going to drown her, in our own pool! Can you imagine that? I got out of there as soon as I heard that. You'll have to ask someone else what went wrong."

Morello sucked on the cigar for a full thirty seconds, then quietly inquired, "How much do they pay you to run that joint, Sorenson?"

"A thousand a month, plus a percentage," the guy replied petulantly.

"How much do I pay you for every little favor I get?"

The guy's response was unintelligible.

"Huh?" Morello insisted.

"You know what you pay me."

"Sure I do. I'm wondering do *you* know."

"God's sake, Tony, stop playing with me. You give me five grand per contact. That's not at issue. I want to know—"

Morello had hauled off without warning and backhanded the guy, sending him sprawling to the ground. The guy just lay there for a moment; then he pulled himself up and resumed his seat.

Morello hit him again, and this time the guy stayed down. The old sadist put a foot on the humiliated man's head and told him, "I don't like you, Sorenson. I never did like you. You're too damn good to associate with a guy like me but you've never complained about the color of my money. Now I asked you a straight question. I expect a straight answer."

Sorenson's voice was muffled in reply but the words were clear. "I didn't kill them, Tony. I don't know who did. I don't know a thing about it. I didn't know anything was wrong until I got your call. I was going along with it. Please believe me. I was going along. I went home and went to bed. I expected to go back to the club in the morning and discover a terrible accident in the pool. Now I swear. I had nothing to do with what went wrong."

"Well now, that's mighty damn strange," Morello said. "Because something went wrong with the other guy, too. He never got to the ship."

Sorenson's head was still beneath Morello's foot. "What?"

"Yeah, how 'bout that. And another two of my boys are right now floating in the fucking lake, just dead as hell. Isn't that strange? Wouldn't you say that's strange?"

"Yes. That's very strange. I swear I didn't know."

"How much did I give you for that guy? All told, how much?"

"About twenty grand, Tony. I'll pay it back. If it went wrong, I'll pay it all back."

"How much you gonna pay me for my four boys?"

"God's sake, Tony!"

"Remember, I don't like you! So you get your ass back where it belongs and you keep it in line. I get the smallest smell of something cute with you, I'm gonna pull your asshole off! You got me?"

"I've got you, Tony."

"Let's make sure."

The bullyboss stood up and put his full weight on the guy's head. Then he savagely jumped on it and walked away without a backward look.

The abused Sorenson did not move. Bolan gave him time to do so; then he went over and checked him out. The guy was unconscious. Blood was oozing slowly from mouth and nose. Patches of skin were ground off the face.

Bolan stood up with a sigh and looked around him. A few minutes more and daylight would be arriving. The meeting was breaking up. He could hear the voices moving along the lawn at the front of the house. A car engine started. He had a pretty good idea who those people were. The war crews—the chiefs, anyway. They'd lost four men overnight. They would not be sitting back placidly awaiting the next loss.

At any moment, someone would be discovering a couple of dead sentries right on their headquarters turf—and there would be a hell of an outcry for sure. Bolan had already spent more time on this "probe" than he'd originally intended. All he had wanted was a feel—a finger on the pulse of Bad Tony Morello.

Well—he'd received that, all right. In spades. As a bonus, the missing chink to the whole puzzle could be lying unconscious at his feet. It could be the first real break in the campaign.

But the numbers were falling away, dammit.

He took a long look at the heavens, then made

43

his decision—kneeling over the fallen man and working at the blood with a compress, inspecting for deeper hurts.

Then he slung the guy over his shoulder and carried him out of there.

Yeah, Susan, Mack Bolan sometimes took prisoners.

And this one was going to pay his keep.

6
PLAYERS

The gray hues of dawn were beginning to push away the night skies as Bolan found neutral territory beside the Morello estate. He eased his burden to the ground and sat down beside him with his back against the trunk of a tree, lit a cigarette, and silently contemplated his prize.

The guy was groaning, swimming toward consciousness.

It came swiftly then, with a twitching of sick eyes as they focused on the figure in military black, those graveyard eyes peering at him from a blackened face. A chilling voice commanded, "Keep it quiet and live awhile."

The guy was tenderly feeling his face with trembling fingers. Bolan gave him a moment to allow the mind to settle before he told him, "The name is Bolan." He dropped a death medal on the guy's heaving chest. "That's your ticket out. It's the mark of the beast, Sorenson, and I'm hanging it on you. So get your breath. In about five seconds I'm going to route a bullet from one of your ears to the other."

The prisoner reached instant panic as the significance of the moment penetrated. He had mouth injuries which made talking painful but the words were clear enough. "Please! Listen! I'm not—I have a wife and two kids! Don't do this!"

"Why shouldn't I?" Bolan coldly inquired.

"Because I'm innocent!"

"Innocent of what?"

"I'm not one of *them*! I'm not . . . a *thug*!"

"What are you, then?"

"I'm general manager of the Pine Grove Country Club."

"Besides that, what are you?"

"I . . . I'm not—"

"Let's understand it," Bolan said, the voice cold and flat. "You're bought and paid for, a slab of meat in Morello's freezer. Now let's go from there. You make me happy, you'll live awhile. But understand. I'm not Tony Morello. I get no kicks from this. I have nothing to prove. I don't need evidence and I don't honor the Fifth Amendment. As you lay there right now, you're a dead man. Only you can change that. Now let's start again. What do you do for Morello?"

The guy leapt to reply. "I guess you could call it recruiting. I recruit . . . business associates for him."

"How do you do that?"

"I, uh, I line them up."

"Let's start again, once more only."

"I set them up!"

"How do you do that?"

"I'm—it's—wait now! I'm just trying to make it

46

clear!" Sorenson's eyes were rolling, seeking. He groaned loudly and put both hands to his head. "God, I think something's broken inside my head."

"I can give you a nine-millimeter aspirin," Bolan offered icily.

The hands came down. "It's better now. What was the question again, sir?"

"We were talking about the seduction of the straight business community, your employers at Pine Grove."

"Yes, okay. Tony needed contacts. I was in a good position to make them for him. Sort of like a broker, you could say."

Bolan commented, "That's pretty heavy brokering, at five thousand a touch." He sighed. "You still don't understand. Now listen closely. This is the way we play this game. I know who you are and what you are. You're a soul merchant, a business pimp, an ugly cancerous sore on your community. That's why you are here. It's why you are going to die, right here. I have not offered you a chance to prove what a nice person you are. That's not the game. I'm offering you the chance to prove how *sincere* you can be. If you were one of those dirty *thugs*, see, I wouldn't have to explain this to you. They know how the game is played. My time is short and my patience very tight. You try the game one more time, *my* way. Start again."

"Okay," Sorenson said feebly. "I set them up. Sex is the bait, usually. Not always."

"Marks."

"Right. Marks. These are very distinguished businessmen. They wouldn't have anything to do with a man like Tony Morello."

"Unless there was a gun at their heads."

The guy took a deep breath and said, "Right. Or

47

an equivalent threat. So I set it up for him. Morello has a funny ship."

"What funny?"

"You know, funny. Girls. Gambling. All the forbidden delights."

"You're not talking about that grimy old freighter, the *Christina*."

"That's all front. I hear it's okay inside. Very nice."

"You've never been?"

"No."

"What are you not telling me?"

"Nothing. I swear. That's all I know."

"You're swearing on your life, guy. What about Susan Landry?"

Those frightened eyes bounced around for a moment before flaring into an understanding. "Oh! You're the one that . . ."

Very coldly, Bolan said, "I'm the one. What about her?"

The guy sighed, very uncomfortably. "Beautiful gal, really. But obnoxious as hell. I didn't know that when I hired her. About a month ago. Very efficient, though. Came on as a dining room hostess. I very quickly moved her up to an assistant manager's spot. She was very good."

The guy was feeling his way. Bolan allowed him the feel.

"I started getting complaints about her from the members. She was . . . always . . . out of place. Poking, prying, snooping around. I caught her in the private files, twice. Said she thought she should know little things about the members, you know, she could handle them better. I told her she wasn't here to handle the members, she was here to serve them. I threatened to fire her the second time. We had a long talk. She agreed to settle down. I let it go. But she kept on snooping. I kept an eye on her. Then she made a play for—for one of the marks. Tried to warn him off, I guess. He told me about it. I had to tell Tony."

"So what was her real interest?"

The guy seemed genuinely baffled. "I can't figure it. I just don't know. Listen—I'm playing the game. You ask, I'll tell. Straight ... honest ..."

"That mark was Judge Daly?"

The guy sighed. "Well, I guess you know it all, anyway."

"Just enough to keep you honest, guy. If Daly tipped you, then why'd he send me out there to save her skin?"

"He did that?"

"That's what I said. How come?"

"I guess I blew it. Overreacted. It probably started him thinking. He was looking very troubled when he left last night."

"You're still playing games, Sorenson."

"I swear!"

"Daly left your place under escort. He didn't go willingly."

"I swear I didn't know that!"

"How many times had he been aboard the ship?"

"Tonight—last night was the first time. But I hear he didn't get there."

"You get five thousand per mark."

"Did I tell you that?"

"I told you."

"Yes. Five thousand per."

"Then why did you get twenty thousand for Daly?"

"Oh, well ... special case. See. He was very skittish. Took a lot of, uh, persistent effort. On my part, I mean."

"He was also very important to Morello."

"I guess so. Yes."

"Let's talk about the other marks. How many. Who."

"Ten or twelve, maybe."

"You can come closer than that."

"About that many. I could run it down by names."

"Let's try it by pedigree."

"What?"

"Business interests."

"Oh. Well I never thought . . . let's see. Tim Conley is big in insurance—industrials, you know. Uh, Hanson—George Hanson—big wheel with the utilities commission. Now this one makes sense: Ben Logan. He's a captain in the Coast Guard. Works out of the district commandant's office, Great Lakes, uh, something to do with law enforcement on the lakes. You want more?"

"I want them all," Bolan assured him.

He got them all, committing them meticulously to his mental file—and he was feeling a bit sick to his stomach, when the list was complete.

He told Sorenson, "Morello I can understand. But you disgust me, guy."

Sorenson closed his eyes as he replied, "Sometimes I disgust myself."

"You knew why Morello wanted chains on those guys?"

"Not at first. I actually thought of myself as a glorified pimp."

"There's no such thing," Bolan said coldly.

"I guess not. Anyway, I started putting it together. Sure. I knew what he was doing. But then it was too late. I was chained, too. Morello is a psychopath. He scares me."

Bolan told him, "It's not the psychopaths that scare me, Sorenson. For a few lousy bucks, a man like you . . ."

"Get off it," Sorenson growled defensively. "I have a wife and kids. I needed those lousy bucks. Don't try to make me feel like something unique. I've been through it all before. I'm rotten, sure, but it's a rotten world, Mr. Bolan."

Bolan got to his feet. "Is that what you're going to tell your kids?"

The battered man's gaze fell to a contemplation of his feet.

"It's a beautiful world," Bolan said coldly. "Don't judge it by the company you keep."

It was full dawn now. Pretty soon the sun would be showing. Bolan took back his marksman's medal and walked away from there, leaving the rotten man adrift in his own rotting world.

Mack Bolan's world was getting more beautiful all the time.

7
ACTION

Morello was pacing the floor of his study like a caged animal, rhythmically squeezing a small rubber ball in each hand as an additional release of tensions, when the house boss, Freddy Bianchi, rapped urgently on the door and poked his head inside to announce, "They found 'im, boss. Wandering down the road."

"Which side?" Morello snarled.

"*That* side. But he's all beat up. I don't think—"

"Don't think! Drag 'im in here!"

The door swung to full open. Bianchi stepped aside. A badly disheveled country club manager lurched through the doorway, propelled from the rear by two of Bianchi's boys. Morello gave him a disgusted glance as he turned his back and went around behind the desk. He dropped into the chair and growled, "Leave him. Freddy—stay."

The two boys went out and closed the door.

Bianchi said, "Front and center, Mr. Sorenson."

The battered man looked around drunkenly, then staggered to the center of the room.

"Look at Mr. Morello," the house boss instructed in a softly scandalized tone.

The guy swiveled about to peer at the man behind the desk. "Sorry," he mumbled. "I'm a little dizzy, Tony. I think you hurt me real bad."

"Get off that sympathy shit," Morello growled, the disgust heavy in his voice.

"Can I sit down?"

"When I say. Where you been, Mel?"

"I don't know, Tony. I guess I was going home."

"Something wrong with your car?"

"I don't know. I'm kind of confused, Tony. I'm all hurt inside."

Morello viciously hurled a rubber ball at the guy and yelled, "I said get off it!"

Sorenson reacted very quickly, ducking and managing to evade the accurately thrown missile.

Bianchi chuckled. "His responses look pretty okay to me, boss," he observed. "I think he's putting us on."

"I think you're wrong," Morello said, staring murderously at the victim. "I think his damn brains are shook. Maybe you better unshake 'em some, Freddy."

Sorenson straightened very quickly. "No, I'm better now. I'm feeling better. What were we talking about?"

Bianchi laughed.

Morello commanded, "Belt 'im!"

The house boss did better than that. He kicked the defenseless prisoner twice in the ass and delivered two ringing open-hand blows to that already battered face. Sorenson let out a shriek and fell to his knees, trying to cover up.

Morello said, "Aw, that hurt, Freddy. You made 'im cry."

"I woke up out in a field!" Sorenson yelled. "This guy was bending over me! I guess he carried me out there!"

Morello got out of his chair and went to the window. He stood there for a moment, hands thrust deeply into pockets, then said, "Okay, sit down."

Sorenson scrambled to a chair.

Bianchi went to the door and stood with arms crossed at his chest.

"He just carried you out there," Morello said, after another moment of silence.

"Yessir."

"Why?"

"I don't know why."

"Who is this so-called guy that just carried you out there?"

"I don't know, Tony. He just—"

"You call me Mr. Morello!"

"Mr. Morello, yes, sir."

"I knew it couldn't be. A punk like you—I knew it!"

Bianchi put in: "It didn't even make sense. Even supposing he *could*. Why break out like that? He could've just got in his car and drove off."

Sorenson's frightened eyes were darting from one man to the other. He cried, "What're you talking about?"

"We're talking about a couple of our boys," Morello informed him with sweet sarcasm. "Laying out in our yard with their eyes bugging outta their head. You wouldn't know nothing about that, huh."

"I *swear*!" Sorenson muttered.

55

"You better know something about something!" Morello growled threateningly. "This so called *guy*—this sounds mighty damned convenient. Don't that sound convenient to you, Freddy? I think maybe the punk *could*, don't you? If he snuck up behind, you know. He could."

"It was Mack Bolan!" Sorenson screeched.

Bianchi's arms came unfolded and fell limply to his sides.

Morello froze momentarily; then he walked jerkily to his desk and sat down.

"What did you say?" he asked quietly.

"I woke up and there he was bending over me. Eyes like ... I can't describe it, you wouldn't believe it. He had on this black costume like raiders wear—like in the movies, all black, even his face was black, like the movies. He had this stuff all over him—this stuff—you know, *war* stuff."

"And what'd he say?" Morello murmured.

"What'd he say? He said he was Mack Bolan. He said I was the mark of the beast."

"The what?"

"The mark of the beast or something like that. He put this medal on my chest, this shooting medal like they say. He said I was laying there a dead man."

The two interrogators locked gazes for a moment.

Morello said to Sorenson, "But here you are, not a dead man. Why not?"

"I convinced him he had me wrong."

"How'd you do that?"

"He thought I was a torpedo or something. Anybody could know better. After I woke up, he just saw that he was wrong."

"He carried you off the property just to wake you up and find out who you are?"

"I guess so, Tony—Mr. Morello."

"Why didn't you tell me this at first?"

"I was scared."

"Scared of what? Scared of the truth?"

"Scared of how it might look to you."

The two locked gazes again.

Bianchi said, "Tell us again what he looked like. Give us a description."

Sorenson sucked in his breath and tried again. "He was all black, he—"

"Not that, dammit!" Morello roared. "Fuck the *black!* What'd he *look* like?"

The confused Sorenson replied, "Well *God*, that's what he *looked* like! A damn black wraith, that's all. Nothing but black and those damn piercing eyes—he scared the *shit* out of me, that's what he looked like!"

"Sounds like," Bianchi said, sighing.

Morello's face had turned beet red. He surged to his feet and grabbed the massive desk with both hands—lifted it, tried to overturn it. That failing, he snatched the desklamp and hurled it through a window.

"Fix that fucking window!" he yelled at Bianchi.

The houseman's face registered no emotion as he replied, "Sure, boss, we'll fix it."

Sorenson was frozen to his chair, hardly breathing.

Morello stormed around the room, overturning tables and hurling small objects against the walls. Bianchi moved not a muscle, nor did his eyes even follow the mad activities in there. When the fit had run its course, Morello returned to his chair and dropped into it with a satisfied grunt.

"Clean up this shit!" he commanded the house-man.

"We'll clean it up, boss," Bianchi assured him, but made no move from the door.

"Get my piece!"

"You want it now?"

"I want it right now!"

The house boss went out and returned a moment later bearing a bulky object wrapped in oilcloth. He placed it gently on the desk in front of the panting *capo* and went quietly back to his place at the door.

Sorenson's eyes were fixed glazedly upon that object.

Morello worked tenderly at the folds of oilcloth, slowly unveiling a submachine gun. A fine film of oil gleamed on the blue metal; wooden stock and pistol grip had obviously been lovingly worked to sheeny perfection.

"What d'you think of this?" the boss asked Sorenson as he held it up for inspection.

"Yes that's—that's a really fine weapon," the dazed man replied in a strangling voice.

"Mint condition, ain't it? I bet I could get ten or twenty thousand dollars from a collector. She's a model 1921A Thompson. It was my papa's. He told me it once belonged to Charley Lucky. You heard of Luciano, right? He and my old man were like two fingers in the same glove."

"It's living history," Sorenson muttered.

"That's right." Morello was fiddling with the ammo drum. "Makes me feel good just to hold it. Sometimes it's better'n a woman. Know what I mean?" He stood up to walk around and perch on the front edge of the desk, directly facing Sorenson. "Mack Bolan, eh?"

The terrified man let out a shuddering sigh and said, "That's what he said."

"Freddy."

"Yessir?"

"You'll have to call Gus and the other tigers. Tell them."

"Yessir."

"I want the ship moved."

"Back down the river?"

"No. Send it north."

"Okay. Right away?"

"Soon as they can. Take the girls off. Put everything away. Get those greenies ready to earn their pasta. How soon can they get steam up?"

"Few hours. We'll have to order the tug. Maybe you should go too, boss."

"Don't get silly, Freddy. When did Tony Morello ever run from a fight?" He patted the gun. "I got my Eliot Ness monster, ain't I?" He chuckled at his joke and waved the muzzle of the weapon in Sorenson's face. "Get it, Mel old buddy? Loch Ness? Eliot Ness? He loved these things, too. Hell of a man, really, no matter what side. Knew a good piece when he saw one, say that. Freddy, you're going to have to tell Gus to safe the corporation."

"Okay, I'll tell him, sure." The house boss was getting that frozen look, again.

"I want plenty of heat. Tell Gus he has my okay to hire all the help he needs, I want full beef at every hot spot."

"Yessir," Bianchi replied woodenly, "I'll tell him."

"Mel old buddy?"

"Yes, Mr. Morello?"

"You're a fucking rat."

"No sir, please—I knew you'd get the wrong idea. I didn't tell him a thing!"

59

"That's why you're alive and not dead?"

Sorenson shrunk deeper into the chair, frozen with fear, no air whatever behind the gasping words: "I told him a fairy tale and he bought it—he bought it!"

Morello laughed. "Mack Bolan bought a fairy tale. Hear that, Freddy? Mack Bolan bought a *fairy* tale!"

The Thompson exploded in Morello's grasp, bucking and snorting in sustained fire, filling the room with its drumming tattoo of death.

The man in the witness chair was literally blown away by the impact, chair and all dancing across the room under the propelling force of the unrelenting hail. Fragments of furniture and window glass shared the stormy atmosphere of that room with gunsmoke and crimson droplets as stark insanity had its way. It did not end until the magazine was empty.

Then Morello chuckled and said, "Well, damn, Freddy. The safety doesn't work. I'll have to fix that safety."

Bianchi had not moved a muscle. He replied, "Yessir, I'll take care of that."

"This room is a damn mess, it's a disgrace. I want you to clean this shit up, Freddy."

And Bianchi replied, "You know I will, sir. You know I always do. Do I have it all? Is there anything else?"

"You can bring that guy Bolan in here."

Bianchi had no reply to that. He'd carefully cultivated the habit of never promising anything to Tony Morello that he could not deliver. And he had no response whatever to that.

8
REACTION

Ben Logan had just completed his usual solitary breakfast and was dawdling at the table with coffee and the morning paper when his housekeeper announced a visitor.

"It's Mr. Christina, he says. And he says it's urgent."

Logan's perplexed eyes regarded the woman around the newspaper. "I don't know any . . ." Then the name registered. He put the newspaper down. "Is Mrs. Logan awake?"

The housekeeper shook her head negatively. "I just looked in on her. She looks just fine."

He said, "Put him in the library, Annie. I'll be along in a minute."

She went away muttering under her breath.

Logan went to his bathroom, brushed his teeth, smoothed his hair, and paused a moment to inspect the creeping gray in there, then went to his bedroom and put on a tie. He also put on a snubnosed .38 revolver, tucking it into his waistband, and buttoning the coat over it. Then he went back downstairs and into the library.

The visitor was standing at the bookcase, idly scanning the volumes there. He was tall, athletic, casually dressed. Something in the way the head was carried, something else about the eyes sent a quick tremor along Logan's nervous system. He closed the door and came immediately to the point. "What do you want?"

The visitor was not all that anxious. "I like your library," he said casually. "You can know a man by his books. I like your books, Captain."

"That's nice," Logan replied coldly. "I'm surprised you could read the titles. What the hell are you doing in my home?"

The caller almost smiled at that. "I like to know a man before I condemn him," he said, in a not unfriendly tone of voice.

Logan's backbone softened a bit. He sighed, took the pistol from his waistband, and tossed it onto the couch. "You're not one of them, then," he said quietly. "So . . . the jig is up. I knew the day would have to come. I've wondered how I would take it."

"How are you taking it?" the visitor asked softly.

"In a word . . . relief. Can we do this quietly? My wife is ill."

"We can do it as quietly as you like," the tall man replied. "How ill is your wife?"

"She's been dying slowly for ten years," Logan said, a bit confused by the personal approach to this most horrifying moment of his life. "Cancer."

"That's hard," the visitor said. "Must be a hell of a fighter to last this long."

"Yes. Thanks. She is. Gallant woman." Logan felt

unreal. "I think she stayed alive mainly for the kids. Now they're grown and gone. I think she's stopped fighting. I don't blame her. Guess I stopped fighting, too. Why am I doing this? I'm not appealing for ... Let's get it over. Read me my rights."

"I'm not a cop, Captain," the man said quietly.

Logan felt his eyes twitching. "You're not a cop."

"No."

"Then what are you?"

The man dipped into a pocket and tossed something toward Logan. It hit the floor at his feet and bounced. Metallic. He bent to pick up the object, inspected it, turned it over and over with his fingers, felt his throat becoming dry, gazed forlornly for a moment at the discarded revolver now so far away.

"So the jig is *really* up," he said quietly.

"Like I said, I like your books."

"Is it okay if I sit down?"

"Please do," Bolan said.

Logan pointedly avoided the couch, dropping into an overstuffed chair near the desk. "I'm suddenly weak as a cat," he confessed. "This is a nightmare. Like getting caught screwing your wife's best friend. Or pissing on the rug."

The tall man had not moved. Now he glided to the desk, raised a leg, perched there casually with one foot remaining on the floor, lit a cigarette, then told his host: "You're not the first. You won't be the last. And it's not too late for you, Logan. You can redeem it."

Logan sighed. "Not quite. I've disgraced the service. I've disgraced my wife and myself. There's no redemption for that."

"Does your wife know?"

63

"God no! That's what it's all about. I couldn't let them—I couldn't—after all she's been through."

"Maybe she'd understand better than you think. She's a fighter. Give her the credit. You're still a young, vital man. How long is it since you've had her loving touch?"

Logan was gripped again by the unreality of the moment. The Executioner, God's sake, Mack Bolan himself was lounging casually in Ben Logan's library offering kind counsel and understanding to the enemy. And the man seemed sincere! Genuinely concerned! He heard his own hollow voice responding to that: "It would still hurt. You should see that film." Logan experienced a deep tremor. He shook himself and said, "God, I must have been bombed out of my skull. I don't even remember going there. I woke up with a naked girl on each side of me. Kids! Just kids—younger than my own!"

"So what did they want from you?"

Logan got up and went to the window. He could not look at the man as he told him, "My job is law enforcement. Does that answer your question?"

Bolan told him, "Not entirely. I'm looking for specifics."

"Then take a look at that damned *Christina*. The registry is Liberian, the crew is Italian, it hasn't left American waters in the past ten months, it's a floating arsenal and a whorehouse and a gambling ship and God knows what else."

Bolan said, "That's interesting. What else is interesting?"

Logan steeled himself to say, "There was a yachting accident on the lake last month. Put that *accident* in quotes, heavy quotes. Supposedly they developed a fire in the engine room. The boat exploded, burned, and sank. Six lives were lost—*six*

64

human lives! My new 'friends' suggested that our investigation should not conflict with my own best interests. It went into the books as an accident."

"Whose boat was it?" Bolan asked.

"Belonged to a local industrialist, Jay Carmody."

"What's his business?"

"I ... really don't know," Logan replied. "He had many interests. Quite a respected man."

"Was he a member of your country club?"

"Yes he was. In fact, he was on the executive committee."

"Was Carmody involved with the *Christina*?"

"Not to my knowledge."

"Is that country club clean?"

"What do you mean?"

"Well, it's quite a collection of power, isn't it? The Cleveland Fifty?"

"We have more than fifty members—and all of the Fifty are not members of our club. Look at me. I'm a member."

The tall man grinned. "You're in about the same pay status as a colonel, right? That's about—what?—twenty thousand a year, counting allowances?"

"That's in the ballpark, yes," Logan replied. "You don't have to be filthy rich to join our club."

"But you have to be very clean."

Logan's eyes dropped. "On the public record, at least, yes."

"Would you like to get clean again?"

"I have very soberly considered suicide, several times."

"That would be the greatest insult you could hand your lady."

"I know. It's why I'm still alive."

"Well . . ." The big man stood up and took a deep breath. "Stay hard a bit longer, Captain."

"You're going to hit this town, aren't you?" Logan said.

"It's already started," Bolan replied quietly.

"If there's anything I can do . . ."

"Just stay clear and keep clean. Can your lady travel?"

"No. She's under constant sedation."

The tall man frowned. "I recommend a move, anyway—in an ambulance, if nothing else. I'm leaning on the boys pretty hard. Morello is very unpredictable. I'd move."

"Thanks," Logan said.

The man smiled and went out.

Logan felt giddy, unreal. But he also felt born again. For good or for bad, a new breeze was blowing through Cleveland.

He heard the front door open and the murmur of voices as Annie let the man out. He went to the window for a parting look. Fine man. Fine. The news stories did not do him justice.

A small car pulled up in front as Bolan descended the steps. Waiting for him, probably—someone picking him up. A young woman—vaguely familiar—bounded from the car, then did a double-take on the approaching man. Tires screeched from another car, somewhere up the street, accompanying the whine of high acceleration as that vehicle leapt into action.

Logan perceived but a blur of motion, but it appeared that Bolan was throwing himself upon the young woman.

Instantly the other car was abreast, speeding crazily and the unmistakable chatter of a machine gun tore finally the peace of that quiet neighborhood.

Logan instinctively hit the floor as his library window shattered and sizzling projectiles hurled themselves through the room.

He did not feel fear. He felt only a terrible desolation. That fine new breeze had died at Ben Logan's doorstep—snuffed out in a hail of bullets.

The giddiness was gone—replaced by the flowing fragment of a famous old sermon contained in one of the books which Bolan had been admiring such a short few minutes earlier.

"Ask not for whom the bells toll ... no man is an island ... the bells toll for *thee* ..."

The entire world had just been diminished.

9
SURRENDER

A minicar pulled up directly in front of the house and Susan Landry popped out of it just as Bolan reached the sidewalk. She spotted him and froze at midstride, obviously startled and confused at finding him here.

Before there was time to even react to that surprise confrontation, Bolan's "combat quick" was activated by a more pressing perception: a hard car leapt from the curb a half block downrange, an ominous black stub protruding from a rear window.

He uttered a guttural cry of warning and launched himself at the girl. Obviously she misunderstood his intent—and even in that flaring moment of crisis Bolan found time to admire her reaction. That lovely face was constricted with fear; still, that voluptuous body girded itself for defense. She pivoted and twirled, evading his initial charge, then came around with a high karate kick—perfectly timed and executed. He deflected the kick with a forearm chop and moved straight into it, lifting her in both arms and propelling the both of them in a flying dive for cover. They hit the turf of Logan's lawn with the girl still securely in his grasp and rolling like crazy toward the safety of a foot-high brick decorative planter. She was kicking and raising hell when the hit car drew abreast and the chopper started blasting.

And then she understood.

The girl melted in his arms, allowing him to take over. He flung her facedown on the grass behind the small shelter and threw himself atop her. Chips of brick and mortar dust showered them as heavy steel-jacketed slugs swept past. She gave a sighing moan and made herself very small beneath Bolan's protection, skirt hiked to the waist, bare thighs trembling in the aftermath of high tensions.

The end was as abrupt as the beginning. The vehicle screamed on along the street, gathering speed as it went, the sound of it quickly fading in the distance.

"Are you okay?" Bolan asked the lady.

She groaned, wriggled clear, sat up, and showed him a rueful grimace which may have been intended as a smile. "It's getting to be a habit, dammit," she said shakily.

"A deadly habit," he assured her. He pulled her to her feet and dusted her off.

She said, "Hey, hey. I can flick my own Bic, thanks."

He growled, "Flick it all the way to hell, then," and spun away to quit that place.

Ben Logan appeared at that moment, the .38 in

hand, a glowing look in the eyes. "It looked like they had you," he told Bolan.

"Felt like it, too," Bolan admitted.

"You're *hit*!" Logan discovered.

He was, but barely. A hot slug had ripped through the shoulder of his coat, taking a trace of skin in passage and producing an ooze of blood.

Landry had just noticed it, also. She said, "Bite my damn tongue. I'm sorry. Let me—"

She was going for the wound. Bolan caught her hand and returned it to her, otherwise ignoring her and telling Captain Logan: "What I said before goes double now. Obviously they had you staked out. They were not there when I came but ... or else they'd picked up on this lady and took this opportunity to go for the hit. You can't risk the doubt. Move it out."

Logan nodded his understanding of that. "Thanks again. I'll do that."

The neighbors were beginning to venture out.

"There will be police. You'd better ..."

Bolan was already moving.

Landry cried, "Well, *wait*!"

It was not a time for waiting. Bolan walked quickly to his vehicle which had been left at the curb several houses down. He got in and kicked the engine. The passenger door opened and Landry slid in beside him.

"Flick my Bic?" she said, smiling.

Bolan showed her a sour grin, said, "Bite your tongue!" and put that place behind them.

The girl was a wild card in Bolan's Cleveland deck. She fit nowhere, belonged nowhere, yet she'd told Bolan in their first meeting that they were competitors. Competing for what? For an *ideal*,

71

she'd told him—which could mean anything or nothing.

Sorenson characterized her as an obnoxious snooper.

Twice, now, Tony Morello's crazies had attempted to snuff her. Why had she gone to Logan's home? Why had she become so flustered upon encountering Bolan there?

And why was she so damned hostile to a man who twice had delivered her from violent death?

Obnoxious, yeah, that was the fitting word. Pretty is as pretty does, lady. Still ... he had to admire her. To be so young, so otherwise totally feminine—and yet so damned *hard*, so self-possessed, so ... what? Ballsy? Right. The lady had balls ... and maybe that was the entire problem.

Bolan was trying to reconstruct her in his mind but he could not pull it together.

A wild card, yeah.

Her voice was small and femininely contrite as she told him, "I'm not that dumb. I recognize the debt. And I'm properly grateful. I can't help it if my damn tongue goes off on its own. I don't know why I say things like that. I don't mean them. I guess it's a defense. I guess I *am* dumb."

Bolan gave her a sidewise glance but that was all.

She said, "You have every right to dislike me. Okay. I accept it. So we *can't* be friends. But there's no reason why we can't be allies."

From "competitors" to "allies," eh?

"We need to pool our resources. You scrub my back and I'll scrub yours."

Thanks, no. Her balls would make Bolan uncomfortable.

"To tell the truth, I don't like you either. You're

a savage and I detest savagery. The only hope for this world is peace and love and gentleness."

Which is why the lady took up *karate*.

"But of course I think I understand you better now. I mean, *especially* now. Your whole life is immersed in brutality. I can see why you would think that brutality is your only answer, why you would feel the need to respond in kind. I mean, you're so caught up in all that."

Yeah, lady. *Dumb* is the word.

"Our differences are not unbridgeable, though. If you could just forget your vendetta until we clear up this mess, if you could resist the urge to shoot everything you don't like ... I mean, you know, if we both *give* a little ..."

She was patronizing him, coming on like an elementary school teacher determined to be kind but firm with the schoolyard bully.

He asked her, "And what are you willing to give?"

She said, "Well . . . cooperation. Friendship. More than that—*camaraderie*."

"And just exactly what does that mean?" he asked quietly.

She batted those blues and replied, "Whatever you want it to mean."

Bolan chuckled and told her, "That is the most unenticing proposition I've ever had."

"Go to hell!" she blazed. "I try to talk to you like a—like a ..."

He said, "Like an equal?"

"You're the most *impossible* man!"

"No, I'm just a man," he said quietly. "I happen to believe that what I am doing is necessary. Not for myself but for you—and for all the millions of others just like you. See, I agree with you, lady.

The only hope for this world is peace and love and gentleness. But you try that routine on that carload of aborigines we just encountered. They were not shooting popcorn balls, you know. And those two sadists last night were not trying to baptize you into holy grace. After the experiences you've had, the average person would have awakened to the idea that we do not live in a gentle world. As for myself, there's no vendetta. I rarely experience any *urge* to kill. But I *can* kill and I do. I have no apologies to anyone for that. Least of all, to you. But I also do not thump my chest in victory over the kill. I am not proud of the kill. I just know for every one I do not kill, a hundred gentle folk—maybe thousands—will never have any hope whatever for a gentle world where love and peace can prosper. You want to be my ally? Then you should know the name of my mission. Eradication is the name, death is the game. The wolves are after the flock, Miz Landry. I intend to kill every damn one of them I can find."

"Every damn one," she echoed softly.

He sighed. "By George, I think she's got it."

"You didn't kill Captain Logan."

"He's a sheep, not a wolf."

"But he's as bad as any. He's allowed himself to be corrupted. He's a police official who is playing along with them."

"He's a victim of the oldest game there is," Bolan explained. "The man is a prisoner of love and nothing else. His shackles are chains of compassion ... for a plucky lady who's been battling cancer for half their married life. Your friends at the club found his single weakness and operated on it like a surgical team—a damned skilled team. Now he dances to their tune, sure, but don't you believe

74

that he's enjoying it. That same surgical knife is now poised at the very heart of that plucky lady. Nobody but Ben Logan is keeping it from plunging in. There's your baddy. Sic 'im, Landry. Go get 'im. I mean, you're so caught up in all that."

Silence reigned in that vehicle for a couple of minutes. Bolan pulled into a shopping center, halted the vehicle, reached across the girl to open the door, and told her, "Goodbye. My advice to you last night is now down for doubles. I suggest you request police protection. I hope you make it."

The girl pulled the door closed. She did not look at him as she said, very small voiced, "I'm not getting out of this car. I'm staying with you."

He said, "The hell you are."

She said, "Yes I am. Please. Let me stay. I promise, no more badmouth, no more lectures. Please . . . Mack, please."

Bolan drummed his fingers on the padded dash, then lit a cigarette and let the smoke out in abrupt little puffs. Presently he told her, "You're sitting in the hellgrounds, you know. They move with me, wherever I go. Aside from the fact that I'm a danger to you, you must understand also that you are a danger to me. You're something else to worry about. Something else to . . ."

She turned glossily sincere eyes to the big stern man beside her and very quietly said, "I guess I'm one of the sheep, too, though. I need you."

"That sounds like a surrender," he solemnly observed.

"That's what it is," she said. "Please. Accept it."

Bolan sighed and eased the car back into the flow of street traffic.

A wild card, sure. So just what the hell was she surrendering?

75

10
TRUCE

Bolan took the lady to another safe house at the opposite side of Cleveland, in the Shaker Heights district.

"Are you parking me here?" she asked warily.

"I'm parking us both for awhile," he told her.

"How many of these places do you have, for goodness sake?"

He smiled and said, "Enough. It's a sad truth of the war, a safe house is safe but once."

"Once used then forever rejected, huh?" she commented. "What, do you come in and scatter these places all over town just on the *chance* it may be needed? Isn't that terribly expensive? For that matter, where *do* you get the money? Your whole thing must be frightfully expensive."

"I have this arrangement with the boys," he told her. "I allow them to contribute to my war chest

77

from time to time. I can't think of a better use for dirty money—can you?"

"Yes, that's poetic justice, I guess. You make them finance their own destruction. You mean you just simply rob them."

"Why not?" he replied, expecting no answer.

"Well, because it's still robbery!" she said indignantly. "Wherever that money came from, it belongs to somebody. It should be returned to the rightful owners."

Bolan told her, "You figure a way to do that and I'll liberate the whole boodle. What is this? You promised no more lectures."

"It's not a lecture. It's an intellectual discussion."

"So screw this into your intellect," he replied coolly. "The Mob is a multinational corporation. Their yearly take exceeds the gross national product of many small nations. Most of it comes in as entirely willing contributions from the working people all around the world—in nickles and dimes from the numbers rackets and the slot machines and sports pools and all the other little games—in dollar bills by the fistful from the crap games and the massage parlors and honest whorehouses, from the bookies, from the juice merchants, from the millions of little shakedowns that go down on the streets of our cities every day—in hundred-dollar bills by the crate from labor rackets, from industrial kickbacks and financial frauds and looted companies. We haven't yet reached the area of thriving casinos, wholesale hijacking, stolen and counterfeit securities, and all the thousands of supposedly legitimate businesses that are strangling competition in the free market. Give it back? You wouldn't find a taker! The poor suckers can't wait 'til payday to contribute more!"

"I guess I've struck a nerve," she said quietly. "I thought you were my nice *quiet* old giant."

He grinned at his own long-windedness and asked, "Quiet what?"

"Private joke," she said. "Never mind. Does this nice safe house come equipped with an honest john? I feel the need to inspect for new possible bruises."

Bolan pointed the lady toward the bathroom and sent himself directly to the telephone for another conversation with his eastern contact.

"I may have something useful for you," Turrin reported. "Judge Daly is semiretired. He has no pending cases. He hears nothing now but those cases falling within his particular area of expertise."

"And what is that?" Bolan wondered.

"Government antitrust prosecutions."

"Uh-huh."

"He's regarded as something of an authority in the matter. His opinions are quoted far and wide, accepted almost as gospel."

Bolan said, "Uh-*huh*."

"Not one of his decisions has been overturned in the higher courts for, oh, years and years."

"Okay, maybe that is something. It's a start, anyway."

"All right. Another item. Morello was kept in a box for the last two years Augie Marinello was alive. Augie considered him unstable and highly dangerous. There was even some talk, at one time—oh, a year ago—of writing a contract on the guy. I told you he was into the distribution of snuff films. Sarge—the guy *makes* snuff films. We know of at least two that came from him."

"Who is *we*?"

"It's quiet but general knowledge here at the headshed."

Bolan said, "Okay. What else?"

"Not much. It was felt for the past year that Morello was trying to find a way out of the box. He's got stuff planted in Phoenix and Tucson. Also a hidden interest in a couple of Nevada casinos. He's also been bankrolling some large narcotics buys via Canada. I guess it's no coincidence that he's coming out roaring now that Augie is dead and buried."

"You mean," Bolan said, "The feeling is there that he's been quietly setting something up."

"Yeah. For at least a year. Oh, I forgot—he's been importing people, too. You know, from Sicily."

Bolan said, "I suspected that. He has a shipload here, now."

"Well, that's been strictly forbidden too, ever since you walloped the last bunch."

"Well, hell, it's a merry-go-round," Bolan commented.

"Yeah, I guess."

The lady had returned and gone quietly to a chair at the far side of the room. She wore nothing but a bath towel, tucked in at the armpits, draping almost but not quite to thigh level. Bolan turned disturbed eyes away from that unsettling sight and told his undercover friend, "Okay, I have company. Thanks for the intel. I'll try to keep you posted."

"One more item, Sarge, if you can manage it."

"Okay, go."

"Susan Landry graduated *magna cum laude* from Ohio State University school of journalism two years ago. She's from a prestigious Ohio family. Her maternal grandfather is Franklin

Adams Paceman, currently one of the big guns in the Ohio legislature. Her father is senior partner in a respected law firm in Columbus, the state capital. The girl has worked on several Ohio newspapers, both before and after her graduation. Most recently she's been unemployed. Her editor at the Plain Dealer said he thought she was doing some freelancing and maybe working as a stringer for one of the big national weekly news magazines; he didn't know which one or even for sure if she was."

Bolan said, "Good work. Nothing at all in very recent history, eh?"

"Nothing at all, right."

"I have to go," Bolan said. "Check you later. Love and kisses."

Turrin growled, "Watch that," and hung up.

Bolan stared at the telephone for a moment, then got up and went to the kitchen, avoiding the girl entirely. He filled a coffee pot and put it on the stove. When he looked up from that chore, she was standing in the doorway with questions all over that pert face.

He put his hands behind him and said, "So. Made yourself at home, I see. Great. We'll have coffee in a minute."

"I thought you were a chocolate freak," she said coolly.

"That was then. This is now. We're having coffee."

She said, "Shove it."

"Bite your tongue," he said soberly.

"You're running, aren't you."

"No. Just resting."

"You know what I mean. You're running from me."

He said, "Okay. What should I be doing?"

81

"You should be looking at my hurts."

He said, "Why should I be doing that?"

"Because you put them there, dammit, and your mirror is not long enough for me to look at them. I could get gangrene, or worse."

"No way," he said. "I already checked them. And I did not put them there. Your swimming buddies did that."

"I mean the new ones."

"Oh. You have new ones. And I gave them to you?"

"You made a tackling dummy out of me, didn't you? Of course I have new ones! You threw me all over the damn yard!"

Bolan chuckled and said, "All right. Come over here and let's take a look."

"You're not going to do it here in the kitchen!"

"Where am I going to do it, then?"

"Well, certainly not here! Not in this damn kitchen!"

He sighed and said, "Where *are* your hurts, Susan?"

"You just go to *hell!*" she raged, and stomped away from there.

Bolan laughed softly and waited for the coffee, then poured a cup and took it with him to the bathroom. The bedroom door was closed. He removed his coat and gunleather, took off his shirt, and cleaned the little furrow in his shoulder.

A journalism major, eh?

He snared a bottle of antiseptic from the first-aid kit and invaded the bedroom. The lady was lying across the bed, atop the covers, bare feet dangling over the edge, the towel totally abandoned and lying on the floor.

He gently slapped the highrise bottom as he sat

82

beside her and told her, "Okay, let's deal. You tend my hurts and I'll tend yours."

Her voice was muffled by the bed but he understood the response. "Go to hell!"

She did have a rather unhappy looking bruise on each thigh just below the highrise. Bolan sighed and returned to the bathroom, wet a towel with cold water, then went back to the lady and ministered some cold-towel therapy to the injured area.

"You have a very interesting bottom," he told her.

"What do you mean *interesting*?" she groused.

"Well, from a masculine point of view."

"You mean stimulating."

"Okay. You're pretty good with words, aren't you?"

"I have a few for you, superman."

"I'll bet you do. And I'll bet you learned them at journalism school."

That beautiful back went rigid. "Wise guy!" she said.

"I thought we had a surrender understanding," he told her.

"Nuts! You didn't accept the damn surrender."

Bolan splashed the antiseptic on his shoulder and tossed the wet towel across the room. Then he stood up and removed the rest of his clothing.

She turned over, looked up at him, and smiled. "Hey," she said, gloating, "I guess I am rather stimulating, at that."

He gently slapped away a questing hand. "We have to get square first."

"Okay," she spat. "You can start by telling me where you found out about the journalism bit!"

"That's exactly where we'll start, Miz Landry," he retorted icily. "Then you can tell me how you parlayed your *magna cum laude* into the Pine Grove swimming pool!"

She came to her knees, batted his hands aside, and flung her arms around his torso, pressing closely with all that voluptuous womanhood.

He growled, "Aw dammit, Susan!"

There were those moments when a war—*any* war—simply had to stand down and make room for the purely human needs of a man for a woman and a woman for a man.

Such a moment was now.

"Let's not fight," she whispered. "Truce. Let's truce."

She was the journalism major, not Bolan—*magna cum laude*, at that—and if she wanted to use the word as a verb then that was quite all right with him.

As it turned out, though, it was more a war than a truce—a glorious war without dishonor to either side—both armies first sending out scouts and recon patrols, then attacks and counterattacks, retreats and withdrawals, maneuvers on the flanks and full frontal assaults up the center, regrouping and girding again and again until both armies were totally expended.

A glorious war, yes, and then the true truce with honor—a warmly affectionate and responsive truce.

"You magnificent giant," sighed the general of the one side.

"*Magna cum laude* with balls," said the other contentedly.

"You beautiful trigger-happy savage. You raped me."

"But that's okay, Peace and Love. You raped me right back."

"Twice."

84

"I owe you one, then."

"Try. I dare you to try."

"God, that's an empty threat if I ever heard one. Who was squawling about her hurts?"

"Who was inflicting them, you sadist?"

"Yeah but who was yelling *charge, charge*?"

"Okay, my scowling savage. That's it for sure. That's the final insult. It's time for another truce."

"I don't think I could stand it," he said tiredly.

But he knew that he could.

There should be, he knew, at least one meaningful truce in every war. Whether verb or noun, yeah—at least one per war. And sometimes two.

11
BRAIN DRAIN

"You can't talk to him right now," Freddy Bianchi advised the caller. "He had a bad night. He just now got to sleep. You give me the word and I'll pass it when I'm able."

"Suits me," the crew boss replied. "He's not going to like this, anyway. I'd rather you tell it than me."

Bianchi groaned. "Okay, dammit, give it."

"I put crews out, like he said. I got everything covered. I had Timmy Zabo and a couple of boys covering the Coast Guard guy. Well now—"

"Did you say you *had*, Gus?"

"Yeh, that's the problem. Tommy's a good boy, you know, but sometimes he has trouble following a bouncing ball. You know."

"Yeah, I know," Bianchi groaned.

"Well, he no sooner than got the guy covered when up drives little Miss Snooper. She drove right

87

past Tommy. He spots her right away. He's a good boy that way, real quick."

"*Too* quick, now, you're telling me."

"This time, yeah. He knew that Tony wanted the broad real bad. So he hit."

"What'd he hit, Gus?"

"Nothing, it turns out. A guy showed up out of nowhere and spoiled the hit. Tommy was a mile down the road before he realizes who this guy probably is. By this time he's on the radio, with me. I tell 'im to keep going and I send another car over for a cool look. There are cops all over. The broad's car is sitting there with about fifty slugs in it. A window has been shot out of the house. A neighbor says nobody got hurt. But this neighbor also says the Coast Guard guy tore out of there before the cops came, says he has a sick wife and a housekeeper in the car with him. We've lost the guy, Freddy."

"Wait a minute, now."

"Worse than that, the broad left with Bolan—and it seems sure to me that both of them had something arranged with the Coast Guard guy."

"Listen. Now listen, Gus. If you think I'm telling that to Tony then you better think again. He already lost that judge and he's plumb sick about that. I mean *sick*, you know."

"It's not for sure he lost the judge."

"Are you crazy?"

"No, I'm not crazy. I checked the hospital no more'n ten minutes ago. They say he's improving.'

"I ask again, Gus, are you crazy? That had blown to hell already. You can't let that guy improve."

"*I* can't let him improve?"

"That's what I said. It's what Tony would say.

You better believe it. You're the tiger, guy—not me. That old guy is going to come out screaming bloody murder. You better put a stopper in that damn quick."

The crew boss sighed heavily and said, "Okay. I'll take care of it. But I don't like the way things are going, Freddy. Suddenly everything is sour. And my boys are all edgy as hell. They know why suddenly everything is sour."

"Don't talk like that, Gus!"

"Hey! What the hell! Why shouldn't I talk like that! It's true. That son of a bitch does it every place he shows. You can't keep a secret like that! I'm telling you the boys are edgy as hell. Frankly, so'm I. What the hell do we look for? *Who* do we look for? There's no name, there's no face, there's nothing dammit until the guy rears up and swats you. Then all you can do is pick up the pieces. And wait for the next swat."

"You want to tell that to Tony?"

"I'd almost rather."

"What th' hell are you saying! That's disgraceful! That's the damndest—"

"Hold it, simmer down. You got it wrong. I'm just saying maybe we should cool it awhile. Tony should get on his jolly ship and take a vacation. We all should. Let the guy roar around town all he likes. The guy doesn't hang around that long, Freddy. He can't afford to. And that's our best defense. We all know that."

"We're talking about *one fucking guy*! You're going to let *one guy* run you out of your own damn town? Gus—that's terrible! I don't believe it!"

"Listen to me, Freddy."

"*You* listen! This ain't the old days. It's not booze and broads you can put on the shelf and come back for when you feel better! This is big stuff! It's Wall Street and it's Zurich and it's Washington! It's all tied together. One damn stagger and it all falls to hell. Do you understand why Tony is under such pressure? Every damn thing he's got is tied up in this! These big men are depending on him to deliver! It's a timetable, it's a schedule—it's push-pull click-click and that's the way it's got to go! Don't start talking about vacations *now*! You've got to stiffen it up, dammit. You've got to get these streets swarming with tigers and you've got to stop that wise son of a bitch in his tracks! Now that's what Tony would tell you!"

"Okay, okay," the crew boss tiredly replied. "You know I will. I was just letting off steam."

"Well, thank God you didn't let it off you know where."

The guy laughed faintly. "I don't have that much steam, Freddy. When Tony wakes up, tell him Gus has got it under control. By that time I hope it's true."

The recorded voices were replaced by a loud hum.

It was the end of a string of recorded telephone conversations.

Bolan punched a button on the intelligence console and turned thoughtful eyes toward his newest ally. "That's it," he said quietly.

"You sound like quite a giant in their book, too," Landry said solemnly. "This is all very revealing, isn't it? It's a good thing you alerted the police about Judge Daly. What was the time on that last call?"

Bolan consulted the electronic display. "Less than an hour ago. We're okay there."

The girl shivered. "I'd give a lot to know the

identities of those 'big men' he was referring to. What was that about Zurich and Washington and Wall Street?"

He said, "The financial-political loop, probably. It sounds like some sort of timetable for moving money—considerable sums, I'd say."

"Could I get a copy of that last conversation?"

He grinned solemnly and said, "For your scrapbook?"

"Is that all it's good for?"

"For you, maybe not. If you don't get into a 'sources' problem. But it would never get into a courtroom."

She said, "Well, I don't give a damn about sources. I'd like to have a copy."

"It can be arranged, sure."

They were, of course, aboard the *Warwagon*. They had made a quiet "pass" of the Morello headquarters in suburban Cleveland and "drained" the collectors installed by Bolan on his first day in the area. The recordings were programmed through the forward console while Bolan tooled on toward the interstate route. They were now approaching the lakefront area.

Landry had been totally enthralled by the *Warwagon*'s surveillance systems—probably as close to "agog" as she would ever get. She told Bolan, "I still don't understand your system. You say you place 'collectors' in the house and then you just—"

He said, "No, the collector is a transceiver. It never goes inside. If I were using bugs in conjunction with the collector, the bugs would go inside. But I haven't yet been able to get inside Morello's headquarters—not inside the building. This tap is on the telephone line itself. Outside the building. It's a countermeasured tap."

"What does that mean?"

"That means that it's rigged to defeat tap detectors."

"This is a whole new world," she said, those eyes glinting. "But now, again, what is the collector?"

"In this case it's a miniature transceiver—that means a transmitter and receiver in a single package—ganged in with a tiny magnetic recorder. The recorder operates at very slow speed. It is sound actuated. That is, it is automatically turned on when a sound enters the tap. It also turns itself off on a time delay when the conversation ends. The transceiver, on the other hand, is impulse actuated from my console here. Upon electronic command, the recorder switches to playback mode and empties its banks at extremely high speed. That playback is fed through the transceiver and, of course, comes out here. It will transmit twelve hours of recorded data in about twelve minutes."

"I don't understand how it can do that."

"The fast replay? You've heard speeded-up tape recordings where the voices sound like cartoon characters? It's the same idea, except that the speedup is so fast that you would hear no more than a high-pitched tone. All of the recording is compressed within that tone. My apparatus here records the tone, then breaks it out into a normal pulse recording. And the whole thing is program coded for time imprints."

"But it's still just a tone recording? I mean, inside your equipment here?"

"Right. That allows greater storage. I have months of stuff in the memory banks. Video, too."

"What?"

"Video. You know, television type."

"Stop, you're blowing my mind. Don't tell me

you can squeeze television programs into a—a tone?"

"Sure. Television is all illusion. They don't send pictures through the air. Not like a still photograph. All those beautiful scenes on TV go through the airwaves as simple electrical impulses. Well, not so simple. But one of these days you'll be able to buy records—you know, like an LP album. You'll just throw the record on a turntable. The turntable will be hooked up to your television set. You'll sit there and watch *The Brady Bunch* from your turntable. The engineers are also developing tape cassettes. Hell, that stuff may already be available."

"And you have video files? Right now?"

"Several thousand items, yes. Mug files, terrain orientation, that sort of stuff. It's computer programmed. Instant access."

"Let's go back to those collectors," she said. "How'd you say you get the stuff out of the collectors?"

"I just have to get within transmission range of the transceivers. In most terrain, that's about a mile. Then I simply push the trigger on the console—and, *voila*, brain drain. It is sucked right in, I have my collection."

"Well, that's very space-agey, isn't it?" she said, awed.

"That's exactly what it is, Susan. Our space probes use very similar gear—or so I'm told."

"It's fabulous. So are you. You're a fabulous guy. Can you accept an apology from a very dumb broad?"

"No," he said. "I sort of liked it better the other way."

"Well, you can just go to hell then!"

"Thanks. I needed that."

She surged forward and snaked a hand inside his shirt.

He slapped it through the shirt and growled, "Watch it! You'll put us in the ditch!"

"Not with that hand, dummy. That hand was just the feint. This hand, *this* hand, my love, *this* is the assault hand."

And, indeed, where she grabbed him that time very nearly put them in the ditch.

He growled, "Okay okay. I accept the apology from the dumb broad."

"Too late," she said. "I took it back. I like it better this way, too."

And the man in the command chair was a very troubled warrior. He was, he knew, dangerously smitten with this unusual young woman. He was, he feared, falling in love again.

Which, he also knew, could be the greatest hazard of all.

12
PACT

They had come to an understanding, of sorts—Bolan and Landry—while lying in torpidly mellow embrace in the safe house at Shaker Heights. He had asked her, "Why didn't you simply tell me that you're a newspaperwoman? It's no big deal."

And she had stirred herself to reply: "For two very good reasons. One, it isn't true. Two, it was none of your damn business anyway."

"It is now. My business, I mean."

"Oh wow. Yes. Isn't it. Okay. I'm not in newspaper work now. Hate it. *Hate* it. Have you ever been in a city room? Noise. Confusion. A hundred people sitting there banging on typewriters. Teletypes clacking and clanging. So I quit. Anyway, I like my freedom. I'm a freelancer now. Better that way. Pick my own assignments. Work my own hours, my own ways. Much better."

"So you are working on a story."

"Sure."

"Back to Go, then. Why didn't you tell me?"

"You kidding? Does an undercover cop tell everybody he meets that he's working on a case? Beside, I had squatter's rights. You were Johnny-come-lately. Also an intruder."

"That's what you meant by competition."

"Did I say that?"

"Uh-huh. You said we were competitors."

"Okay."

"That left the territory wide open," he told her. "You became an unknown quality. I live in no-man's-land, remember. Sometimes it gets a bit tricky identifying friend and foe."

"Awww. You thought I might be a *foe*? Really?"

He said, "There were those moments, yeah."

"How 'bout now?"

He punched her weakly on the thigh. "Worst one I ever tangled with. I think you've severely undermined the war effort."

"Call me Delilah," she said contentedly.

"How did you tumble to the action at Pine Grove?"

She snuggled closer. "I'm being interrogated, aren't I?"

"Something like that, sure."

"Oh well. I guess you want the whole truth and nothing but."

"Try your best, huh?"

She giggled. "There had been this series of violent deaths in the area. Nothing called murder, though. Accidents. Suicides. And all of them in high society. People were getting paranoid. Then it stopped. And everyone was saying the usual clichés about, you know, tragedies running together and that sort of thing."

"It stopped six weeks ago," Bolan said.

"Okay, smarty. If you know it all . . ."

He told her, "I just felt that somehow it related to the problem here. But I couldn't run down the connection."

"Well, of course I knew nothing about your problem here. I was simply sniffing around. Journalistic curiosity, you know. And I came upon something. It took me straight to Pine Grove Country Club."

"What'd you come upon?"

"A list of names. A typewritten list of names. Twenty names. All of the accident and suicide victims were on that list. Or they had been. A line was drawn through each of those names."

"Pine Grove," he reminded her.

"First let's have a moral understanding."

"Okay. Whatever that means."

"It means that I refuse to be an accessory to murder. Anything I tell you is privileged. You can't use it. For—for target practice."

"Back to that, huh? Okay. I respect your sensitivities. But you'll have to respect mine, too. You call it murder. I call it duty. We'll have to reach some technical understanding somewhere between those definitions. And I agree that I will not murder anyone whose name comes to my attention from your privileged disclosures. Okay?"

"Sounds like doubletalk to me, Sir Giant. You promise me that you will not *kill* anyone."

He said, "You know I can't do that. I'll do my duty as I see it. Understand it, Susan. I'm not speaking of justice. I'm wearing no blindfold. I don't have the rigidity of a cop or, say, a prosecuting attorney or a sitting judge. My task is to identify the enemy and then eliminate him. If I—"

"And you'll eliminate every wolf you find."

"Every one I identify, yes. But I am very discriminating. I pick my targets with the greatest of care."

She shivered and put a few inches between them. "It sounds so cold-blooded."

"Would you rather the blood be running hot when I make the cut? Would you trust the result better that way?"

She said, "I just don't see how you can take it upon yourself that way."

"Someone has to," he replied grimly. "I just happened to be the guy who was standing there with nothing else to do when the duty roster was posted."

"That's ridiculous!"

"I wish it were. But it's not. Susan, I want you to give up journalism."

"Go to hell."

"Seriously. You should find a good man, get married, and stay home where you belong."

"You've got to be pulling my leg."

"Sure I am. But let's say I'm serious. What would you say?"

"I'd tell you to go to hell. I take pride in my work. I'm good at it. Some day I'll have a Pulitzer. Tending house is not exactly my idea of the best way to utilize four years of very expensive educational preparation. What I'm doing is very important. Just as important, and maybe more, than being the Great Earth Mother."

He said, "Okay. Apply that to me. I have *twelve* years of very expensive education. At the time I left 'Nam, I represented a U.S. government investment of several hundred thousand dollars. I am among the most highly trained and specialized soldiers our nation has ever turned out. I am rated as expert with every personal weapon in the national armory. I can also modify, build, or design weapons of fantastic complexity. I could show you a hundred and one ways to kill a man without putting a mark on him. I have developed a photographic memory. I can live for days without food or water or sleep. I can navigate by the stars and I have night vision almost equal to that of a jungle cat. I can hear a twig snap at a hundred yards in a living jungle and I can tell you the make and approximate horsepower of an engine passing by on land, water, or in the air. I could write a training manual on explosives and I could damn near do it for electronics surveillance devices. I could also write a textbook on military tactics and strategies. I have been highly trained to detect the smallest anomaly in terrain, costume, or personal behavior—and I've had plenty of opportunity to develop that training to a fine art. In Vietnam, one of my standard missions was to penetrate enemy-held territory, locate and identify civil and military leaders, and eradicate them. And they all wore black pajamas."

"That's all highly impressive," she murmured.

"It isn't given to impress. I'm trying to impart an understanding. You're telling this guy, now, this trained military machine, to go home and tend house. I'm telling you that I cannot do it. The enemy is the enemy, dammit, whether in Europe, Asia, or Cleveland. They all wear black pajamas. There's no one around who can or will distinguish between the sheep and the wolves. Well, dammit, I can. I don't enjoy it. I wish to hell there was some way I could justify it to myself if I simply turned away and let someone else worry the problem. But everywhere I look, Susan, I see wolves stalking sheep. It isn't something I can simply turn off. I *see* it, dammit. And I have no alternative but to respond. So I take a practical approach. You call it cold-blooded. Okay. Pragmatics are always cold-blooded. Wars are cold-blooded. You cannot fight them sensibly any other way. So I do not respond hotly, flailing away willy-nilly at an occasional wolf as it struts past. I use my training. I plan my campaigns. And I'm killing wolves."

She said, "Well, I see your point. I wish I could applaud it. Oh hell. The truce is ending, isn't it?"

"Not necessarily. I don't want applause. I simply want cooperation. How did you tie in your list with Pine Grove?"

She sighed, wriggled, scratched her chin, then told him, "Well, the rat tried to get me killed, anyway. Another name was penciled at the top of that sheet of paper. Mel Sorenson. He's the manager at Pine Grove. It was no feat at all to track that."

Bolan told her, "I spoke to Sorenson a few hours ago. Please note that I did not execute him. No need to. That guy wrote his own script when he threw in with the likes of Tony Morello. If it will ease your wounded ego, and just for the record, Sorenson did not think that Morello would hit you. Was Judge Daly on your list?"

"Yes. I tried to warn him. That's how I got undone."

"Where'd you get that list, Susan?"

"Sorry, that definitely *is* privileged info."

"Okay. I'll respect that. For now. What did you think the list represented? What did it mean—to you?"

She flipped a hand in the air. "It blew my mind. It suggested so many things. But of course there were logical, rational explanations too. I mean, you know, harmless ones. They were all members of the country club. The list could have been prepared for any number of reasons. Special treatment, maybe. Naturally, in that view, there was nothing particularly ominous in the fact that expired members had been deleted. But I sure smelled a story. I had to check it out."

"So you went to work at the club."

"Yes. Twice I got called on the carpet for my curiosity. I didn't really learn anything. In fact, I was just about to shelve the whole thing. Then I overheard Sorenson in a conversation with Tony Morello. Hey, I'm not naive, I knew who Tony Morello was. I worked the police beat in this town for about six months. From the drift of the conversation, I got it that Sorenson simply *must* deliver Edwin Daly to that nefarious floating whorehouse—*that night*, or else."

"You knew about the *Christina*, huh?"

"That sort of thing does get out, doesn't it?" she replied. "Everybody in Cleveland, it seems, knows about the *Christina*."

Bolan asked her, "So what is your reading of that list of names now?"

She lifted a knee and tenderly inspected it. "Sounds like blackmail, doesn't it?"

He asked, "To what end?"

"I thought blackmail was an end in itself."

"Not always," Bolan said. "Very often it's simply a means to a much larger end. It's standard procedure for the Mob. If you need them, buy them. If you can't buy them, terrorize them. If they're too large to terrorize, eat them."

"And what if you can't eat them?" she asked softly.

"Then you remove them. And hope for better luck with their successors."

She said, very faintly, "Oh."

"Somebody has a very ambitious program in mind for this area."

"Sure," she said. "Tony Morello, I told you."

"Tony Morello is a stumblebum. This one is beyond his scope."

"I think you're wrong," she told him. "But I'd like to tag along and find out. Can I tag along?"

He said, "I usually try to avoid war correspondents. They give away too many secrets."

"You can trust this one. You know me. I'm ethical. I protect my sources."

"It is a combat area, you know," he reminded her. "Things could get very hot. In fact, they will."

"I've had my baptism," she reminded him. "And I promise to be a good girl."

"I'm in charge," he warned her. "You do what I say, when I say it. There's no democracy on a battlefield. I lead, you follow."

"Okay. I accept that."

And that was how Susan Landry came to be in the *Warwagon* with Mack Bolan on that very grim morning in Cleveland. He had known from the beginning that it was a mistake, that a woman had no place in his war, that she would be in very grave jeopardy.

But, then, she already was.

This way, at least, he could keep an eye on her. And that was becoming a more and more pleasant exercise with each passing moment. Too pleasant, yeah . . . much too damn pleasant.

13
HEART DRAIN

The Port of Cleveland nestles inside a long break-water which stretches from Gordon Park south-westward to Edgewater Park, subdivided into East Basin and West Basin. Sharing the protected lake-front are several yacht clubs, a small airport geared for personal and business craft, public areas, and the port terminal.

Bolan nosed the *Warwagon* into a public access area and told Susan Landry, "It's time to go to work."

He went to the midships console and fired up the intelligence computer, then plugged in the data he'd acquired during the preceding hours. Next he put through a hookup to the National Data Center in Washington, using radiophone via the Bell System and a confidential access code.

"What are you doing?" Landry inquired,

watching all the activity from behind Bolan's shoulder.

"Going to Washington," he said. "It's time to identify some wolves." He produced a plasticized card and scanned the program codes imprinted there. "There we go," he muttered, more to himself than for the lady's benefit. "Corporate structures, American and multinational."

She said, "I don't want to believe this."

He poked in the program code and asked her, "What's the problem now?"

"You actually *do* have government connections."

"No more than anyone else could have," he told shall all things be revealed unto you. Even to you, her. "All you need is the proper equipment and a will to know." He turned to smile at her. "And then Peace and Love."

"I don't like it," she chafed. "You're telling me that anybody—just *any*body—can plug into the private lives of people all over this country?"

He said, "By George, she's got it. Hush a minute. Here it comes."

An eight-by-ten viewscreen in the onboard computer came alive and began displaying line after line of electronically imprinted information. The speed with which each line appeared and vanished could have been entirely bewildering to the untrained observer; not so to the man at the console. He was totally absorbed in the flow, eyes unblinkingly assimilating the rapidfire display, occasionally grunting with approval at something he saw there.

A minute or two later, the viewscreen went black. Bolan muttered, "Well I'll be damned."

"I hope it meant something to you," the girl commented. "It's all totally lost on me. Don't you get a printout?"

"I don't have space or need for hard copy storage," he said. "It's all in the onboard computer now, anyway. I can recall it any time I need it."

"You really do have a photographic mind, don't you?" she murmured. "That's almost frightening. I'm still hung up on the damned information leak, though. I suppose you could just poke my name in there and get my life story, couldn't you?"

He nodded. "Everything that's been a matter of public record. Give me your Social Security number and I'll show you."

She said, "Thanks but no thanks. So what did you learn this time from your Washington connection?"

He told her, "I plugged in the list of names from Pine Grove. In a corporate program. You would not believe the creeping tangle of interests there. I'm going to have to think on it some."

She said, "I didn't give you that list."

"No. But Sorenson did."

"Thanks, pal."

"Confidence works both ways, little buddy."

"I haven't withheld anything important," she protested.

He smiled. "Neither have I. What do you know about explosives?"

She blinked. "All I want to know. Nothing."

He went aft to the armory and opened a special, safelike box. The girl wandered back and asked him, "What are we blowing up?"

He produced a large package of doughlike substance wrapped in black waxy paper. "They're scheduled to move the bad *Christina* at noon. I don't want them to do that."

"Hey!" she cried. "You can't blow up a ship in dock. It could take the whole port with it!"

105

"Right. That's why I am not going to do it. I could sink her, though, right where she sits. Without disturbing anything around her. I could almost do it to that old tub with a can opener. But then that would litter the port, wouldn't it? Interfere with shipping. So what can I do, Peace and Love?"

"Call the Coast Guard," she muttered.

"They couldn't hold her. What's the violation? Foreign registry severely limits the guard's jurisdiction. That's mainly why so many American-owned vessels register with Liberia. They can get away with most anything. So. What do we do?"

"You're baiting me," she said uncomfortably. "You know what you're going to do."

He said, "Yeah," very solemnly. "I'm going to drop her screw."

"Drop what?"

"The screw—the propellor. The thing that makes her go."

"I know what a propellor is," she said, small voiced. "A ship that size must have an awfully large one. You're going to blow it off, eh?"

"Uh-huh." He was making strips from the doughy package. "Wrap a few pounds of this around the shaft. Add an impact detonator. Soon as the shaft makes a turn, that screw will drop. Part of the shaft, too, if I'm lucky. A kink or two, anyway."

"It sounds very risky," she said worriedly.

"This stuff is pretty stable," he assured her.

"No, I didn't mean—won't someone see you?"

He grinned. "Sure. Invisibility is not one of my talents. The trick is to make them see what I want them to see. And I won't be able to use scuba gear."

"Will that stuff work underwater?"

"This stuff will work anywhere. Actually it's used quite a bit for underwater demolition work."

"You're making me nervous," she said, and went forward.

Bolan completed his preparations and carefully coiled the strips of plastics into a small metal box. Then he changed clothes—donning Levi's and sneakers and a blue dungaree jacket, topping off with a black knit navy watchcap. He then placed a Schmeisser autopistol and several clips of spare ammo inside another box and carried the stuff forward.

Landry was seated at the midships console, staring gloomily at the apparatus.

"Stay put," he commanded. "I'll be gone maybe an hour. Don't show yourself and please don't mess with the gear."

"And what if I'm not here when you get back?" she asked soberly.

"I'll wonder how you got so dumb. And I'll say a prayer for you."

"Goodbye."

"Goodbye, Susan."

"Don't kiss me."

"I hadn't planned to."

"Why not?"

"Because you're obviously disturbed again."

"I'm not disturbed."

"Stay put," he commanded firmly, and departed.

Later, he would wish that he had kissed her.

The *Christina* was bustling with preparations for getting underway. Dockside connections for power and water were being terminated. Last minute supplies were being taken aboard. The bridge was manned and seamen were scurrying about the decks. A couple of cute kids in shorts and halters were watching the activity from an after railing on the boat deck. Bolan scowled at that. A telephone conversation recorded in the *Warwagon*'s surveillance banks had specifically ordered that "all the girls" be taken ashore. Obviously these two did not fit the classification. Where then did they fit?

Smoke was pouring from the stack. The tugboat was maneuvering to come alongside. Linehandlers on the main deck of *Christina* were jawing goodnaturedly with the tug crewmen, heavy Italian accents in abundance.

Bolan waited until the tug was secured; then he pulled his runabout alongside the tug, tied to, and leapt aboard. The tug's skipper turned to him with pleasant curiosity.

"How long before you move?" Bolan inquired.

"Probably ten minutes," the guy replied. "What's up?"

Bolan made an unhappy face. "I gotta go down and inspect the damn screw."

"Well, you better do it damn quick. What? Like that? You got no diving gear?"

"Just a quick look," Bolan explained. "It's not worth all that."

The guy was looking him over. "Well, you got plenty of time for a quick look." He laughed. "Don't hang on too long. They'll be turning those screws soon as we clear the dock."

Bolan laughed back. "That's why I checked you first. Don't do no turning 'til I get outta there."

"Wahooo! Ride 'em cowboy!"

They laughed together and Bolan went back to his boat. He cast off and sent the little craft on toward the overhang of the fantail. Very funny, yeah. The "screw" of a ship this size would have a diameter larger than Bolan's height.

He kicked off his shoes and strapped the metal box to his waist, then slipped over the side and into the water. It was cold, yeah. The propellor shaft was submerged by about ten feet. The water was clouded, visibility poor. He spent a minute sizing the job, then surfaced for air. The tugboat skipper was looking his way. He went down again, hooked his legs about the propellor shaft and sat there for stability while working the plastics in. He had to surface twice again before the work was completed. By this time, the guy on the tug was visibly agitated.

Bolan pulled himself into the boat and returned alongside the tugboat.

"Find something wrong?" the skipper wondered worriedly.

Bolan panted, "I thought so at first but naw, it's okay, I guess. Tell the captain the shaft is getting pitted pretty bad. He'll be wanting that looked at next time he goes to the yard."

The tugboat skipper casually saluted as Bolan pulled away. He heard him relaying the "inspection" results to the bridge of the *Christina*. The guy up there laughed and said something in Italian.

Bolan laughed too. Yeah, he laughed inside all the way back to the public pier—wishing he could have hung around until *Christina* turned her screw.

The inner laughter ended, however, the moment he entered the *Warwagon.*

He'd been gone about forty minutes.

He wondered how long Landry had been gone.

There was nothing left of her here save a note pinned to the command chair: "I need to check

109

something out. I memorized your phone number. Contact you later."

It was signed "Peace and Love."

"I wish you that, kid," he muttered to the empty gunship.

Somehow it had never seemed so empty before.

14
ASPECTS

Bolan did not expect Susan Landry to contact him again. She had left because she simply could not stomach what he was, could not come to terms with it—perhaps did not even wish to. So okay. Good for her. He would not wish that she compromise her own deeply felt principles. Not for the sake of a living dead man, for sure.

But the event of her departure gave the man considerable pause, nevertheless, causing him to call to question once again his own deeply held convictions. Was he in fact as wrong as Susan believed him to be? Did it even matter, anyway, this insane war between an immovable object and an irresistible force? Hadn't the shit machines simply reassembled themselves everywhere he'd smacked them down? What had he actually bought, in real human terms, with all the bloodletting?

Suppose she was right. And suppose everything

Mack Bolan had committed his life to was but a hollow mockery of what a *real* life should be. Was Mack Bolan the supreme sucker, in reality a pathetic throwback from some long-vanished age of mankind, like some of the columnists had said?

Bolan caught his own eye in the rearview mirror and was startled by what he saw there. Only then did he realize that his eyes were wet.

Damnation!

He was sitting there feeling sorry for himself! And for why? Because some zit of a girl, some pompous kid with pedantic principles did not like his innards?

Well, to hell with that!

He bade farewell to Susan Landry in his mind and in his heart, savoring the memory of a few hours pleasantly spent, but consigning the differences which had split them to a higher level of understanding. And then he turned that brilliant military mind back to the problems of his war without end.

He pulled to a clear area to take a reading on the Port of Cleveland. The bad *Christina* was wallowing near the sea gate, now under tow by two tugs which were assisting her back to her berth. Bolan smiled with grim satisfaction and pulled onto the Lakeland Freeway, running northeasterly. It was high time to jerk a couple of tails and get this Cleveland game on the front burner. The intelligence scan from Washington had raised some disturbing questions, some of which perhaps would never yield to an Executioner-style bust. Questions of corporate hanky-panky aplenty in this "best location in the nation" and which, if answered affirmatively, would make Tony Morello's goon squads the most underrated *gestapo* in the whole world.

112

It was a far larger game than Bolan had initially suspected. And, yeah, perhaps too large for a lone soldier to tackle effectively. It seemed, though, that he had come upon the game at the best possible time. If the recorded hysterics meant anything, the "corporation" was at a crucial stage of development. Perhaps then a bit of heat, strategically applied, would boil their pot over and the cannibals would end up eating one another. Morello was already showing signs of cracking. A couple of good hard pushes could conceivably produce a domino effect throughout the Cleveland conspiracy.

The *Warwagon* took up a southerly track at Gordon Shores. Bolan fired up the forward console, remoting the onboard computer to the con. He summoned a terrain display with city sector overlay and poked in digital conversion for all of those names on the Pine Grove hit list. Red blips immediately began pulsing at various points of the overlay. Those red blips identified the hot spots—those locations where the "corporation" needed to be "safed."

Bolan was looking for a fight.

And he knew precisely where to find a dozen of them.

"I wouldn't be a cop for all the money in China," the wheelman grumped. "Imagine just sitting around like this day and night, forever, just watching and waiting."

"They got no money in China, Hoppy," said Johnny Carmine, the crew chief. "All they got is people and rice."

"That's what I meant," Hoppy groused. "And I still wouldn't take it. I don't like these stakeouts, Johnny."

"He don't like these stakeouts," Carmine said to the two behind him, swiveling about in the seat to flash them a grin.

Both guys laughed nervously.

The wheelman snorted, "What the hell they laughing at? They don't know a word you said. How'd we get stuck with these damn greaseballs anyway?"

"Aw, they kapish what they need to kapish." Carmine snapped his fingers and said, very softly, "Guns!"

A chopper instantly appeared at each rear window, safeties clicking ominously.

Carmine nudged the wheelman and said, "See? All I gotta say now is h-i-t and you better pity anybody in sight. Don't sell these boys short, Hoppy. You could've been one yourself if your grandpoppa hadn't got the American itch and come to better pasture." He sent a hand signal to the rear seat and the choppers disappeared from view. "These boys got the itch, too."

"Wish they'd do their scratching back on the ship, then," the wheelman growled. "They give me the creeps."

"You might be damn glad they're not on the ship if that guy shows up around here."

"That guy ain't gonna show up around here! What th' hell!"

"We never know, Hoppy. We just never know."

Carmine stretched himself and picked up the binoculars.

"Whataya see?" the wheelman asked a moment later.

"Same old shit," Carmine replied, sighing. "Nothing in and nothing out. The joint is as quiet as

114

Christmas night. I bet that guy is sitting in there shaking his ass."

"Think he knows we're out here?"

"Nah. Why would he? But he's probably scared to death the bastard will show up. Or maybe not. I wonder do these guys really know what's going down."

"I wouldn't know," the wheelman said. "Ask your friends back there, the spaghetti suckers."

"Hey, I'm getting a little sick of that shit, Hoppy. You lay offa those guys, dammit!"

"Okay okay."

The wheelman's attention became attracted by something in the rearview mirror. "Something's coming," he announced.

"It's an RV," Carmine said, using his own sideview mirror. "This is a funny neighborhood for an RV, isn't it?"

"You see 'em everywhere nowadays," the wheelman said, though his attention was still riveted to the approaching vehicle.

It was a GMC motor home ... very difficult to see into ... some funny kind of smoked glass for windows....

The big rig was moving slowly, hesitantly, as though the driver was looking for something. It pulled directly abreast of the hit car, halted very briefly, then pulled on ahead and went to the curb a hundred or so feet ahead.

The wheelman snarled, "Well, that goddam prick! He's blocking our view!"

"Simmer down," said Carmine, tensely. "Let's see what."

A guy stepped out of there and looked around a bit uncertainly. He wore blue dungarees and jacket like a guy in a cigarette commercial, cowboy hat

115

and all. In his hand was a small paper bag, neatly folded at the top like a lunch sack, only white like a baker's bag.

"He's gonna have a picnic!" the wheelman snarled.

"Shut up! Keep your eyes open!"

The boys in the back seat were shifting about, unable to follow the conversation but aware of the tensions in that vehicle.

The guy was walking back along the street toward the car. An unlit cigarette dangled from his lips. As he approached, the wheelman lowered his window and yelled at him: "Don't leave that damn thing there in my way like that!"

The guy came on, halted at Hoppy's window, peered in, touched the brim of his hat, and announced, "Howdy. I'm looking for 3215."

"You won't find it in here!" the wheelman snarled.

"What is this, meals on wheels?" Carmine asked nastily.

"Beat it, cowboy!" Hoppy commanded officiously. "You're interfering with a police surveillance!"

The guy said, "Well, ten-four, good buddies, mercy me, threes on you." He leaned into the vehicle and flipped the paper sack past the wheelman's head and into the back seat, very casually, then took off at a fast trot to the rear.

Hoppy growled, "What th' . . . ?"

A guy in the back grunted, *"Che cosa è—?* [What is—?]"

Carmine yelled, "No! Throw it—!"

Too late came the awareness.

Both Carmine and the wheelman were electrically scrambling for that "lunch bag" when the

116

whole world turned red and puffed itself out to impossible dimensions, fracturing eardrums and bursting horrified eyes, rending flesh and fabrics and metal all as one in a consuming burst of the fragile bubbles of life.

And even after all life had departed that tortured scene, the forces of holocaust raged on through the twisted debris, finding new fuels to feed the devouring flames.

Later, an official observer would declare: "We can't even determine how many people were in that vehicle, not yet. That's a job for experts. As for the cause of the explosion, we can only state at this time that a very powerful device erupted in the interior of the vehicle. The blast seems to have been centered in the rear seat area and it engulfed the entire car. The trunk lid was blown thirty feet away. We, uh, discovered also in the ruins the metallic remains of several weapons, including two light submachine guns. We, uh, are pressing the investigation into that aspect."

The official statement did not include the information that a military marksman's medal had been found lying beside the smouldering wreck. The police were, uh, pressing the investigation into that aspect, also.

15
COLLECTION

Bolan understood Morello's gameplan. Indeed, he would have anticipated it even without access to the telephone instructions issuing from that headquarters on the Cuyahoga. The guy was obviously following the convoluted logic that a strong defense is the best offense. He had placed headhunters on surveillance stakeouts covering each name on the Pine Grove pigeon list, evidently assuming that Landry or Sorenson or both had provided Bolan with the names. He was not "protecting" those people so much as he was using them as bait for the counterattack. There was nothing wrong with the logic, as long as the planner would assume that two could play the same game at the same time. And it was a game which Bolan understood very well, from both sides of the question.

His second strike of that fated afternoon came less than twenty minutes following the first. Gerald

Parma and crew were staked out in view of a factory office near Washington Park. They had already been alerted to the fact that Johnny Carmine's unit was not responding to radio calls and that "something might be up." The four men in Parma's vehicle were tense and jittery. Nevertheless, they sat unalarmed and watched a tall man dressed in farmer's overalls step from a line of trees which bordered an open field and casually approach their position.

At about fifty yards out, the man stopped and released a strap from the corner of his baggy overalls, turning away from the men in the car and stepping off on a diverted course.

Parma was on the radio at the time. He reported to River Base: "A-OK here. Nothing but a farm boy looking for a place to whack off."

His wheelman commented, "They ain't no farms around here, Jerry."

The gunner behind Parma cried, "Watch it!" and grabbed for his chopper.

The "farm boy" had whirled about with a stubby weapon raised and sighted. Parma instinctively threw himself toward the floor, mistaking the weapon for a sawed-off shotgun. It was not a shotgun but an M-79 grenade launcher hefting a 40mm round of high explosive. The weapon puffed and the HE round impacted on the doorpost, beside which the rear gunner was scrambling to get his own weapon lined into a firing angle. He never got there. The explosive force of the strike rocked the heavy vehicle and engulfed it in a raging fireball. The two men in the rear were killed instantly. Parma was screaming weakly from the front floorboards. The wheelman had been ejected by the blast and flung clear with his clothing ablaze. Another puff from fifty yards out sent a second firestorm into the stricken vehicle, this one impacting just forward of the firewall and instantly stilling the cries of human distress. Ruptured gasoline carriers ignited an instant later and the entire vehicle was briefly airborne by the resultant secondary.

The flaming wheelman appeared at the shattered nose of the vehicle, on all fours and wheeling crazily like a performing elephant. A different weapon immediately boomed from fifty yards out, dispatching a sizzling mercy round of instant death. The human torch fell to his side and continued burning. The man in the overalls stood quite still for several seconds, obviously assessing the human situation over there—then he holstered a big silver pistol, shouldered the M-79, and quickly walked away from there.

He struck again ten minutes later, this time in a sedate residential neighborhood farther east. Billy Centennial and crew never saw what came for them, though all died with guns in hand. Something crashed through the rear window of their stakeout vehicle, instantly filling the interior with a choking gas. As the gasping men tumbled from the car, an unseen automatic weapon chattered its song of eradication, sweeping all four off their feet and depositing them in a heap at curbside.

The Executioner was at war.

And now the entire city of Cleveland knew it.

Bolan released the sector display and turned the *Warwagon* toward River Base. There was little point to an endless succession of firefights at the periphery of the problem. He had made all such strikes that had been intended. It was time now for an assessment of the results of this "push" against Tony Morello's delicate sensitivities. But he did take time, first, to stop at a public telephone for another contact with Leo Turrin, reluctant to use the mobile phone for such purposes.

He got the little guy on the line and told him, "Well, I think the thing is rolling now. Do you have any late poop for me?"

"I checked out that country club," Turrin reported. "Can't find anything against it. But, Sarge, you were right about that Cleveland Fifty. Most of them are represented there. That's a hell of a congregation of firepower—even if it is for fun and sun. You know how much business is conducted in this country over gin and tonic?"

Bolan replied, "Yeah. I'm just beginning to find some of the strands. I think they're tied together in a Gordian knot. Alexander the Great cut his with a sword. I might be faced with that same decision, Leo. I don't mind telling you that I'm dreading it. Have you heard any rumbles?"

"Nary a one. But it's not surprising. I told you. Morello has few ties in this town. Whatever he's doing, he's doing it without the rest of the company. Listen. About that Gordian knot. You watch your ass, buddy. The feds have been going easy on you. You raise too much ruckus in the civilian community, you're liable to have Brognola howling up your ass again."

"That's the worst of my worries, Leo," Bolan growled.

"Well. I didn't notice any politicians with balls in that Cleveland select. You better look outside. They damn sure need a political base if their aim is high."

"That's what bothers me," Bolan told him. "I still

haven't identified all the players. All I have right now, in fact, are pigeons."

"Just what do you think is going down there?"

"I feel that my subconscious knows it all," Bolan replied in a musing tone. "It just hasn't reached the conscious levels yet. Tell me, though. Have you seen a long-range weather forecast recently?"

"Weather? I doubt it. No. Why?"

"The weather people are warning that we might have a record winter on tap this year."

"So? The energy crisis is all fixed, I thought. Are you thinking of those Flag Seven nuts down in Texas? Are you getting echoes?"

Bolan said, "I don't know. And the energy crisis is not fixed, no. Smoothed over for awhile, that's all. Suppose we did have a record winter. I mean, suppose the temperatures went below zero and stayed there for a month or two. The entire industrial northeast in deepfreeze. What's the fuel reserve situation for this region? Is there enough oil storage? Are our natural gas reserves adequate?"

"Are you asking me?"

"Yeah, I'm asking you."

"Okay. I'll try to find an answer. You're onto something, aren't you?"

"Maybe, maybe not. It sounds too crazy, too big, too impossible to even consider. But I was wondering if it might be possible for some smart operators to corner the energy market in this area."

"I wouldn't think so," Turrin replied. "That stuff is pretty heavily regulated. What are you onto?"

"I don't know. I'm just thinking out loud, I guess. But I did a scan on the corporate crossovers in this region. Covering only the principals whom I know are involved in Morello's game, one way or another. It's a fantastically complicated study, buddy.

A real bag of snakes. And everything I touch smells like gas."

"Gas?"

"Yeah. Natural gas, liquified gas, heating oil. Every facet of its existence—from drilling to refining to transportation to storage to marketing and all the stops between. Even a number of small gas reserve companies have been absorbed by several of these outfits recently."

"Like I said, it's a heavily regulated industry."

"So was alcohol, Leo, in the nineteen thirties. What the hell does that prove? As long as *people* do the regulating, then hell . . ."

"Well. I'll look into that hard winter for you. Anything else?"

"Find me a kinky politician, Leo. A fatcat with local interests."

"I could probably find a dozen without leaving my chair," the undercover fed wryly replied. "Your, uh, your judge—your corporate judge—how's it look?"

"I doubt that he ever got into it. I doubt that he knows a thing."

"But there is an angle there."

"The angle is there, sure. They wanted the guy bad."

"Well, there you go, talking about regulation. If that is the gig, then you can bet they'd try to cover all bases."

"Yeah," Bolan said quietly. "That's what I'm betting. Thanks, Leo. Hit you later."

"I'm always there," the little guy sighed and hung it up.

Bolan returned to the *Warwagon* and found the mobile phone signaling for his attention. He stared at the instrument through a moment of speculation, then pulled on a sneer, picked it up, and said, "Who'd you want?"

It was Susan Landry—confused at first and a bit breathless. "I want—I thought—this is Susan, Susan Landry."

Bolan responded to that in his natural voice. "Fancy that."

"Well, I told you I'd call."

"I didn't believe you."

She sounded as though she had been crying. "I want to come home. I'm fed up with peace and love. I just want to get back into that hot little car and help you with your collections."

He checked the time as he asked her, "Are you okay?"

"I'm fine, yes. The hurts are all gone."

He frowned. "Are you some place cool?"

"Yes, I'm fine." There was a long pause, then she asked, "Can I come home?"

The Bolan frown deepened. "I think ... we should leave it the way it is, Susan. We agreed to meet at midnight. Let's have it that way."

Another pause, then: "No, please. I can help you with your collections. Can you pick me up right away? I'm at a shopping center on Snow Road—Brookgate." Another pause. "I'll be at—"

He said, "You know better than that. I'll set up the meet. I'll call you back in ten minutes. Give me the number there."

"I—I can't give you this number." Pause. "I just borrowed the phone. I'll call you back. Ten minutes?"

"Ten minutes," he said grimly and rung it off.

The *Warwagon* was already in motion and he was not far from his goal. His mind was seething with the certain knowledge that the lady had made

125

that call with a gun at her head. She'd managed to tip him to that—a damn classy lady—and she'd also *maybe* managed to let him know where she really was.

She'd really wanted to help him with his "collections."

Yeah.

He hit the retrieval area and immediately summoned the intelligence. It came in on a forty-second tone and settled with a hum into the program bank. He poked in the time noted earlier, during the conversation with Susan. And the playback was an echo: "Who'd you want?"

"I want—I thought—this is Susan, Susan Landry."

He shut it off and ground his teeth and forced his mind to settle down. But all he could think of was a madman who killed for kicks and invented hideous tortures for idle diversions—and a beautifully classy lady with textbook ideals about peace and love, a tear in the eye, and a sob in the voice—and what she must have been put through to divulge that telephone number.

Eyes that oozed ice watched the digital clock in the console—four minutes to wait for the next call—while hands that had learned to kill coolly and methodically twisted at the fabric of the combat fatigues, impatient now for a kill that would be anything but cool.

The Executioner was awaiting a very personal collection. And God help Tony Morello if he did not find her alive and well.

16
NEAR MISS

The call came right on time. Bolan scooped up the instrument and said, "Yes, I'm here."

Her control was much better now. She asked, "Where do I meet you?"

"Can you make it to Edgewater Park in fifteen minutes?"

Pause.

"I—I think so, yes."

"Okay. At the lagoon. Be there. I won't wait."

"Will you be driving the hot little car?"

He said, "What else. Hurry. You just missed a collection."

Less than sixty seconds later, the first big crew wagon nosed out of the estate and headed toward town, followed by three others in quick succession. Bolan had each one close up in the optics as it cleared the gate and made the swing onto the road. Each was packed to the gunwhales with hardeyed men. But nowhere in there did he spot Tony Morello or Susan Landry. Which was something of a surprise. He had half expected that they would take the girl along as a spotter or decoy. But of course there was no reading the Morello mind at a time like this. And Bolan's gameplan had remained entirely flexible. He was playing strictly to the ear, hoping only for a chance to reach into their midst and snatch that lady back safe and sound.

And maybe this way was better. Morello must have severely weakened his palace guard by sending out those head parties—four vehicles, eight men per—yeah, severely weakened.

Bolan was preparing the EVA even as his mind worked the problem. Within a minute after that last vehicle cleared the gate, the warrior was in the armory selecting his weapons. He stripped to the combat blacks and slipped on the battle rig, a belted configuration including grenades, smokers, and incendiaries. Big Thunder, the .44 AutoMag, went to the right hip and the Beretta Belle at the left armpit. Finally, the big punch combo—an M-16 assault rifle with an M-203 nestled below, the mated designation for the M-79. This "big punch" provided a combination of a 5.56mm machine gun with a 40mm hand cannon, the latter handling loads of high explosive (HE), smoke, gas, or buckshot as the need demanded.

Within two minutes after the departure of the head parties, Bolan was out of his vehicle and running for the wall of the Morello estate, the "big punch" slung across his chest from a neck harness. He hit the wall at full charge and vaulted over, landing on his feet and continuing the charge with hardly a break in stride—in the garden area where he'd stalked Morello and Sorenson in the dark,

128

where now was bright daylight and a startled sentry in mind-boggling confrontation with a real live commando on the hoof.

The guy spun away from that charge with a grunt of fear, frantically attempting to reach a shotgun which perhaps only moments earlier had been propped against a nearby tree. He hit the ground on his back, scrabbling hands clutching the shotgun at the same moment that a black pistol in the invader's hand spat silently on the run to chug nine millimeters of sighing death splattering into that constricted throat, a warning cry caught there and pinched off in the dying gurgle.

Bolan charged on.

Another guy in the parking area looked up just in time to see the second flaring of that silent weapon and to intercept another sighing missile. This one yelped audibly as life departed, bringing another guy down off the porch with bugging eyes and a handgun springing from sideleather. Bolan ran right over that guy, clubbing him with the Beretta and crushing the larynx with a well-placed kick as he danced on by and leapt onto the porch.

Another gawked at him from the open doorway. He sent nine millimeters sighing ahead to clear the way, smacking in at forehead center and punching the guy onto his back and sliding in his own fluids.

It was an old house with a wide central hallway, huge sliding doors leading off to either side, all dark woods and musty odors, a stairway climbing off directly inside the door.

A handgun yapped at him from above, three quick slugs pounding into the floor near Bolan's feet. He stepped under the stairwell and dispatched forty millimeters of HE straight up. The big round hit the ceiling up there and blasted on through, sending back a mushroom of fire and showering debris. A section of second-floor railing crashed to the main floor with a smoking body in tow. Bolan followed through with a prolonged burst from the M-16, adding splintered wood and plaster dust to the flames up there. Pounding feet and urgent voices told the story of panic in the palace.

A shaky voice up there called down, "Ease off, ease off! You can have it!"

"Bring it down!" Bolan commanded icily. "Hands on the head and moving spryly!"

They came down with surprising spryness, horrified gazes stuck to the big angry man in black.

"Out the door and don't look back! Quickly! Quickly!"

There were three of them. Bolan snared the tail man and shoved him ungently against the wall. "The lady!" he growled.

"Downstairs I guess," the guy gasped. "Basement." Scared eyes showed the way.

Bolan shoved the guy on out the door, with the advice, "Tell your *amici* to keep it moving all the way to hell." The guy hit the ground running.

Flames were spreading through the upper floor when Bolan located the basement stairway. Lights were on below, and he could hear someone groaning painfully. It was an L-shaped stairway with a landing halfway down. He sent a machine gun burst into the wall at the landing, then quickly followed with his own presence there.

Nothing came at him.

A man's body lay at the bottom, only the torso in view. "Don't shoot," the guy groaned. "It's okay here. Don't shoot!"

Bolan cautiously descended the stairs. It was

130

okay there, yeah. Large, open room with plenty of height. A movie studio—or it had been, once. Now everything down there was just torn to hell—couple of expensive-looking cameras, studio lights, couple of beds, couch, a kink rig with wrist and leg irons, sound equipment—all of it bullet-riddled and reduced to junk.

The guy on the floor was Freddy Bianchi.

Both legs were practically cut away from the guy just above the knees. He'd been shoestringed with an automatic weapon.

Bolan coldly said, "Dammit, Freddy, how'd you get that?"

The guy was trying to get a belt around one of his thighs for use as a tourniquet. And he was in hellacious pain. "Gimme a hand," he pleaded.

"I want the girl."

"She ain't here. Help me."

Bolan shoved the muzzle of the M-16 against the guy's throat. "Okay," he said quietly.

"Look, I'll tell you! But do something, dammit! I'm bleeding to death!"

Bolan knelt in the guy's blood and silently went to work on him. A moment later he told him, "Okay. Maybe you won't bleed to death. But I think you're going to lose those legs, Freddy. Maybe not, if you get quick help. Who did it to you? Morello do this?"

"He finally flipped completely out," Bianchi groaned. "Crazy as hell. He's crazy, I tell you."

"Tell me something new," Bolan suggested. "Where's the girl?"

"He took her. Lammed out right behind the boys. Back way. I tried to tell 'im. Keep the girl for bargains, case it goes to hell. Aw naw. Wrong thing to say. He got it into his head. I saw it, I saw it getting there. Wants to make her a star."

Bolan growled, "What?"

"Yeah, a snuff star. You know how that goes."

Bolan's raging gaze took in the shattered studio. "Why all this, then?"

"You figure it," Bianchi said. Those eyes were rolling up, the pain and shock having their way there. "He's got a better one on the ship. Probably going there. That's where I'd look, Bolan. And I hope I'm right. Hope you kill the crazy bastard. Do me a favor. Shoot 'im in the crotch. Let 'im bleed to death through his prick. You'd never believe the shit I've took off that maniac. Then he does this to me. Shoot 'im in the prick."

"This is going to hurt you, Freddy," Bolan said. "I have to get you out of here. The joint's on fire." He hefted the guy the most painless way possible and started up the stairway. Smoke puffed down on them.

Bianchi groaned, "Take the back way. Cellar door—leads outside."

The big double doors had already been flung open and left that way. Morello's way out, no doubt, with something very precious to Mack Bolan under tow. He carried the shattered man up the stairs and into the fresh outside air.

The old joint was going fast, flames leaping high above the rooftop. There were no signs of lingering personnel on the grounds.

Bolan took his burden to the front sector, well clear of the burning building, and left him in the grass beside the drive. "I owe you, Freddy," he told him before he left. "I'll send help, depend on it."

"Shoot 'im in the prick," was the last thing Freddy Bianchi said to Mack Bolan.

And, at the moment, Mack Bolan could have cheerfully done so.

The real anger—the deeper anger—was at himself, though. He had allowed himself to be programmed by personal feelings, and he'd just kicked the whole Cleveland campaign down the drain . . . for nothing, probably. For a cocky kid who would not accept the rules of the game, who'd gone off blind and headstrong to slay dragons the gentle way . . . refusing to believe that there was no gentle way.

So he'd loused up the entire game. The only handle he had was going up in flames. The only inside man was now far ahead and scurrying to his "impregnable" hardship.

And Bolan knew. He'd lost the game. He'd lost the girl. Morello had won both. A lunatic had turned the trick at Cleveland. Bolan knew, yeah, because he was aware that he'd screwed up more than the River Base hardsite. During that agonizing wait for Landry's second call, he'd killed the time with a listen to another recorded conversation from the latest collection.

He was such an expert in everything, sure. So why hadn't he known that *Christina* had *twin* screws. In that murky water, how was a guy to know—unless he'd taken the time like an expert should to look up the nomenclature for that old scow? Personal feelings again, yeah. His mind had been divided, too fragmented in the need to justify himself to that cocky twit of a girl. So he'd dropped only one of *Christina*'s screws. A bit crippling, sure, but not absolutely disabling. A few minor repairs, and she was getting set to limp out again at four o'clock.

The time was now three-fifty.

In another few minutes, the lunatic and the cocky twit would be on their way "north" in a warship. And she *was* a warship, with more than a hundred foreign savages ready and willing to repel boarders. More, and worse, she boasted a "movie studio" where cocky twits could be reduced to shredded, shrieking, mindless flesh while the cameras recorded for sicky posterity the total disintegration of everything human.

Bolan halted tiredly at the door to the *Warwagon* and raised pained eyes to cosmos.

She was not a twit but a lovely young woman with a mind of her own and the courage of her convictions. But even if the "twit" had fit—and no matter what the fit—he could not abandon her to that, whatever the cost to himself or to the world at large.

Something very cold, and very deadly, and very determined was settling into the Bolan psyche.

He had lost Cleveland, okay.

But he had not yet irretrievably lost everything else.

And, by God, he would *not* lose *any*thing else. Not even a twit.

17
PHASED

Bolan pointed the battle cruiser toward blood and
threw caution to the winds, contacting his friend
Leo Turrin on the mobile phone.

"This is Striker. I'm on the mobile so watch it."

"I gotcha. It's okay here. You sound hot."

"I am. I suggest you call Wonderland [Washing-
ton] and tell the man to get set for another crisis.
I'm about to attack a foreign flag vessel in U.S.
waters."

"I guess you know what you're doing," Turrin
commented solemnly.

"Not really. I'm just doing what must be done.
Tell the man she's a gunship with a pirate crew.
That could help. If she goes down then she needs
to be raised, combed, and exposed for what she is.
There's a man here who can help. He's cooling it
somewhere right now but I'm sure he'll come out
when the heat is gone. I'd rather not name names

on this open loop. Tell the man I'm sending an electronic program on Channel Zebra. He'll recognize the help when he sees the name and pedigree. The guy is clean for my books and I trust him. Tell Wonderland I said that. Also—"

"Hey, uh, this is beginning to sound like a post mortem memo."

"Yeah, isn't it," Bolan said grimly. He sighed into the transmitter and added, "Way the ball bounces sometimes, buddy. A wild card turned up in my deck. Scrambled the play here pretty badly. I'm just trying to recover what I can."

"Let it go," Turrin urged. "Kill the play. Save it. Bring it back another day."

"Can't do that," Bolan told him. "That wild card is a warm one. The wildman stole it. I have to steal it back."

"That kind, eh! Uh-huh. Same one you mentioned this morning?"

"The same, yeah."

"Maybe I have something that will change your mind."

"Not hardly. What do you have?"

"We were talking about fatcat politicians."

"Yeah. I'm too late for that, Sticker. I've blown it."

"Maybe not. Remember when I gave you the rundown on your wild card? The pedigree, I think I said, was very prestigious."

"What are you saying?"

"Wonderland ran a check on the grandfather. Looks clean on the surface but there are deep shadows on the X-rays, buddy."

"X-ray any politico, Sticker, and you're apt to find shadows somewhere in the background."

"Yeah, but these are in the foreground, Striker.

136

Get on a clean line and I'll give you the startling details."

"There's no time for that now. You'll have to give me what you can right here."

The little guy sighed heavily into the long-distance connection. "How do I put it? There's very good reason to believe that the grandfather is your fatcat. I could mention a couple of committees in a certain seat of government which this guy controls also, which could give a lot of credibility to that *smell* you were talking about. If you get my meaning."

"I get it, thanks," Bolan replied, the voice suddenly very weary.

"What I'm saying, pal, is that you don't want to believe everything you may read in a wild card."

"I get your meaning. Thanks."

"Are you okay?"

"Yeah I'm fine. I was just thinking of something. Uh, thanks for the info. It doesn't change anything. Not unless you can offer absolute proof that I've been conned by a very clever twit."

"Guess I don't know what a twit is but it doesn't matter. I have no *proof* of anything. But the nose gets accustomed, you know."

"Yeah, I know. Hey. Light a candle, huh?"

"It's already burning," Leo said, and signed off.

Bolan mechanically worked another combination and sent his file to Washington. Only one man had the retrieval code and that man was Harold Brognola, top cop in the Justice Department. There was nothing "official" in the arrangement. In fact, Brognola would be in serious difficulties if his involvements in Mack Bolan's war should become known. But the two men worked together, each scratching the other's back in their unofficial joint war on organized crime. If Bolan should not survive the night, then "Wonderland" would at least be privy to his findings on the Cleveland scene. And maybe all would not be lost, after all. From the tenor of Leo's report, the head fed was already boring into the Ohio problem.

And of course the meaning was plain *vis à vis* Susan Landry and her maternal grandfather, one Franklin Adams Paceman. If the guy *was* the political front for the Cleveland Pipeline ... then Bolan could no longer accept anything concerning his understanding of Susan's interest in the proceedings as valid.

A journalist, looking for a "story"?

Or a secret watchdog looking over the goodies in madman Morello's jurisdiction? And why not that? Everyone who'd ever dealt with Morello knew that the guy was unstable. His own organization had once contemplated a contract on his life.

There were, of course, an endless list of scenarios which could be developed around that lady.

None of them meant a damn thing. Not in this present situation. Whoever and whatever the lady may be, Bolan was absolutely certain that she was in the gravest of all possible circumstances. There was but one scenario to be developed in that vein. And Bolan knew that one well. Far too well.

No, Leo, it didn't mean a damn thing.

The bad ship *Christina* was going to meet Mack Bolan.

First, though, there was a fated appointment to be kept with Morello's headhunters. He wanted those guys out of the picture, no matter how the rest of the thing turned out. Too many atrocities had already been visited upon Cleveland's straight

138

community by that Gestapo force. Men such as Ben Logan could not be abandoned, either.

He found them where he knew he would, bracketing the lagoon of Edgewater Park with their war chariots, chafing under the wait, and beginning to conclude that their quarry was not going to show. The vehicles were spaced out about fifty yards apart, in communication by radio—and Bolan had them in his monitors.

"He ain't coming, Gus."

"You let me decide when he ain't coming, Harry."

"Maybe we got the wrong place. Maybe he already came and went."

"Maybe you worry too much, Rocky. Sit tight and keep the eyes open."

"Did she say a Jaguar, Gus?"

"For the third time, Bobby, it's a red Jag with a white top. Now let's keep it quiet!"

Bolan threaded the needle between the two point vehicles and eased on along the drive. It was an artificial lagoon, formed by a natural jog in the coastline at one side and the extreme southwesterly extension of the breakwater. Sea gates provided access to both Lake Erie and the West Basin. A yacht club shared the marina area with public facilities. A charter boat had just returned a fishing party; otherwise there was very little activity in evidence. Bolan could see the ore docks directly northeast and the entire Port of Cleveland sprawling out beyond there. And he could see *Christina*, at that moment clearing the gate that separated east and west basins, moving slowly under her own propulsion.

And it was strange, Bolan once again reflected, how the tangled threads of universal cause and effect always seemed to be busily working just beneath the surface of things, setting stages and manipulating wires to produce those inexplicable happenings which men called destiny. Because this place, this lagoon, was probably the only point in the entire port from which he could hope to launch an attack upon that fleeing vessel. Yet long before he was aware that such an attack would be coming, he had set the task doubly hard by also dispatching Morello's entire remaining hardforce to that selfsame point.

He sighed, wondering just how smart the human mind really was—wondering, also, if somehow his subconscious had peered ahead to that very point of time and space, bringing all the scattered pieces together for a final climactic and perhaps cataclysmic resolution to all of Mack Bolan's problems. He could not have done it better with the computers, had that been the intent.

So be it.

He sent the *Warwagon* around in another pass and punched in a readiness check for the fire systems, activated the forward con, brought in all the optics, cycled the launch platform doors to standby, brought all the systems on the line, then wheeled about to confront the enemy.

They were in a double slot, paired sets, manning the road from inconspicuous watchpoints at either side, two at the point, two at the flanks. He could not risk a rocket attack—too much civilian community at the periphery, too much possibility of bystander involvement.

The fishing party was straggling away, climbing into vehicles and departing.

A guy down near the water was folding a blanket and walking away toward the yacht club.

And the enemy . . .

"What's that guy in the bus doing?"

"Not a bus. It's a . . ."

"It's not a red and white Jag, is it? He's looking for something, though. Maybe just something to warm his bed . . . but . . . Rocky—take a couple of boys down there and check it out."

"He's moving again, Gus."

Indeed he was. Bolan had opened the smoker chute and was making another pass of the combat sector. Timed flares rolled out at precisely spaced intervals to fall inconspicuously into the grass beneath the slowly moving vehicle.

"That bus is up on the damn grass!"

"Call a cop then."

"Cut out the jawing! Watch 'im! Just watch 'im!"

The enemy "watched 'im" make a complete circuit and return to the starting point.

"Okay, Rocky—look 'im over! And *good*!"

A door on a flank vehicle open and a couple of guys tumbled out. At that moment the smokers erupted, sending dense black clouds spiraling across the combat zone. The two guys on EVA drew up damn quick, gawked, then spun about and hurriedly returned to their vehicle.

The radio monitor sputtered, "Jesus Christ! What's that?"

"Let's get outta here, Gus!"

"He's come! The guy's here somewhere!"

"Keep your heads, dammit! It's just smoke! Don't make a move 'til I tell you!"

The entire area was now behind the smoke barrier, with the winds coming in off the lake and moving it steadily against the enemy as the flares continued to pour it out. Bolan slung two ammo belts from the neck and descended with the big punch combo at his chest. He could see little better than they but he was trained for this sort of exercise and he needed to see very little; he had their numbers and their emplacements firmly etched into the combat consciousness.

And he took Rocky the flanker first, with forty millimeters of roaring destruction head on, following immediately with a blazing sweep of chattering tumblers. Two guys emerged stumbling from that flamesplit blackness, only to be met by a figure-eight wreath, and returned to the fire.

Bobby the pointman was leading his force in a pell-mell evacuation of their emplacement, when forty flaming millimeters erupted in their midst to send bodies flying with greater alacrity. Then another and another in rapid succession. The vehicle huffed and rent the blackness with a towering fireball, revealing the other point vehicle with good old Gus backing cautiously along the macadam strip.

There was but a glimpse of horrified faces behind that windshield, gaping at Bobby's unhappy fate, then the M-16 split that windshield in a left-to-right crossing. The vehicle arced onto the grass, only to be followed there by an explosive round that rocked it onto its side and another that smacked into the exposed underside, touching off another explosive source and lifting the shredded remains on a pillar of burning gasoline.

The fourth car was moving recklessly out of the trap at high speed, the wheelman obviously driving by instinct alone. Bolan heard the whine of the engine above all other sounds of that tortured combat zone and moved quickly into the intercept. He lifted the weapon and let one fly, targeting purely by the ears. The miss was by about six feet forward, as revealed by the flash of the hit—but the next round was dead center on the hood ornament of that speeding vehicle. It lurched and spun into a tree and burst into flames. Bolan sprayed those flames with a full clip of 5.56; then he turned quickly and walked back across the smoky hellgrounds.

It was not a "clean" hit, no. It was sloppy as hell, right. Doomed voices inside that madness were raised in anguish and fear. But the damned would just have to take care of their own. Mack Bolan had other needs in mind. The moment would not wait.

He cleared the smoke zone and returned to the battle cruiser. Several civilians were running up from the marina, attracted by the sounds and sights of warfare. Others were beginning to show from the area of the yacht club. Very quickly there would be an official reaction.

At the moment, no one seemed to be giving any attention to that "recreational vehicle" poised at the background of madness. Well and good. The next phase of the climactic battle of Cleveland would span mere seconds of time. Bolan had no wish to compromise the "cover" of that fabulous battle cruiser. With all eyes turned to the first battleground, perhaps he could get off his launch without spectators to the event.

And there would be an event.

Oh yeah.

She was still well within range.

And the *Christina* was going to meet Mack Bolan.

18
BANANAS

If the computer systems could be regarded as the *Warwagon's* brain, then the rocketry would certainly be her big fist. Utilizing a swivel-platform retractable rocket pod concealed beneath roof panels, the system is operated from the command deck and features greatly sophisticated fire-control equipment with night-bright optics in conjuction with laser-supplemented infrared illuminators. Target acquisition is electronic and automatic and can be programmed through video or audio sensing systems. Once acquired, the "target lock" is unshakable. Each of the four "on-line" rockets may be preprogrammed in advance for individual targets anywhere within the 360-degree target horizon. Control options include manual fire, auto fire via time or video-motion activators, and EVA (extravehicular activity) remote manual. The system delivers massive destruction at impressive range and with pinpoint accuracy, whether the target is stationary or moving.

Bolan would be lying in his secret heart if he did not acknowledge that the rocketry was the crowning grace of the entire weapons system, its primary reason for existence, in the same sense that a B-52 exists for the single purpose of dropping bombs. And yet he used those rockets with the greatest discretion and sometimes downright reluctance. They were not weapons to be unleashed willy-nilly, without thought for their awesome destructive capability.

That consideration was heavy on his mind that grim afternoon in Cleveland as he cycled the platform to "raise and lock" and meshed in the onboard computer for fire control takeover. Redly glowing rangemarks superimposed themselves on the optics monitor as he scanned the bad ship *Christina* in search of vitals. He did not desire to sink that ship, though he felt that he easily could. Her hull was of paltry quarter-inch steel and welded seams, nary a bolt in the whole bucket. German subs during World War Two had sent many of her sisters to the bottom using nothing but deck guns, loath to waste torpedoes on such sitting ducks.

He could sink her, sure. But that was not the intent. He merely wished to disable her, to panic her, and then to board her. So he selected his targets with care, electing to minimize mortal damage and going for pure panic effect.

She was well clear of the sea gate now, limping along at a brave four knots and obviously maneuvering with a bit of difficulty, the heading almost due west. That latter was a bit of a surprise. Bolan had expected her to point her bow due north to

146

move with all possible haste toward Canadian waters. Later, perhaps, she intended to do so and was now simply "shaking down" the imbalanced propulsion close to shore.

All to the better. He had her wheelhouse in perfect three-quarter profile. And that was the prime target—the brain, all the control functions. He cycled in all four birds, set up the automatic sequence, and punched her off.

The first firebird rustled away on a climbing trajectory, seeking altitude in a computerized path and trailing flames and smoke behind her. Number two leapt away in a quick following, roaring along in fast pursuit, followed immediately by three and then by four.

The platform automatically retracted into the roof.

The Fire Sequence illuminator flared out.

Target One grew intently red then flared out also, replaced by an amber pulser.

Bolan did not need the optics monitor to verify that strike. A firestorm enveloped that wheelhouse out there, puffing smoke and flying debris high overhead.

Target Two flared out.

Another bright flash highlighted the bridge deck just abaft the stack.

Target Three flared. . . .

Bolan had seen enough. He opened the warchest and took out a packet of money then grabbed a raincoat and shrugged it on over the combat rig. He pulled the *Warwagon* into the yacht club parking area and stepped down. No one was giving him the faintest attention, all the interest of the moment remaining up in the hellgrounds.

A man of about fifty was frantically tying up a

sleek inboard cruiser, impatient to get to the hellgrounds to see what was going down there.

Bolan took the line from the man's hand and replaced it with the money packet. "I'm buying it,"
he said.

The man was staring stupidly at the money. "It's
not for sale," he protested.

"There's enough there to buy three just like it,"
Bolan told him. He stepped into the boat and cast
off, kicked that fine engine, and took her out of
there. The former owner was still watching him as
he cleared the breakwater and opened her wide.

Bad *Christina* was in bad trouble.

The entire superstructure from the boat deck up
was aflame. She had lost steerage and obviously
someone in the engine room had retained sense
enough to stop the engines. She was wallowing,
her bow pointing back toward the Port of Cleveland, and great frenzied activity was erupting all
about those worried decks.

Two lifeboats had been lowered by the time Bolan got there and someone had also lowered the
gangway. Guys were in the water all around, some
in life jackets and some not. Others were lining the
rail and crowding the gangway. Chaos was afoot
with push and shove the prevailing mood. People
were yelling at Bolan in Italian and a couple began
swimming toward the craft.

He ran alongside the gangway and tossed a line
over. No one took it, all too intent upon leaping
into that lifesaver. Bolan gave it to them and
fought his way to main deck, tossing several guys
overboard in the effort. None challenged his right
to board. If any ship's officers were alive and
aboard, none were in evidence. Most of these men
were not sailors at all but hired foreign guns sud-

denly without viable sponsorship. The one or two obvious sailors whom Bolan could spot were being overwhelmed by the panic moving those others.

Bolan moved on up to the cabin deck and began kicking doors. The fire was one deck above and beginning to spread downward. A guy in a steward's jacket lurched around a corner and yelled something at him in Italian. Bolan grabbed the guy and asked, "Morello—where is he?"

"No parlare Inglese!"

"To hell with *Inglese!* I want Morello! *Morello!*" He made like an old-style movie camera. *"Cinema,* Christina, porno!"

The guy got that. "Ah, porno! *Sì, Don* Morello."

Bolan desperately tried his flawed Italian. *"Dove è Don* Morello?"

The steward's eyes wavered as he muttered, *"Ponte due."* He twisted free and took off running.

Bolan did not parley the *ponte* but *due* he knew as "two." Deck two, maybe. That would be ... below decks.

He found the ladder and descended on the run—main deck, first deck, second deck—and hell, he was practically in the bowels of the ship. Which was exactly where this place belonged. A "movie" set, sure—and what a set—straight from the annals of the Marquis de Sade—chains and stocks and every kinky device a confused mind could dream of.

But no Morello.

He heard a groan and went deeper into the foulness. This had been a cargo hold, originally. Large. Plenty of overhead. A curtained area contained an editing table and paraphernalia, projector, small screen. A director's chair was placed beside the projector. The projector was warm to the touch. He heard the groan again—much closer now—behind him!

A bulky object, draped in a black satin sheet and lurking in a darkened corner of the projection room. With shrinking heart, Bolan removed the drapery.

And, yeah, it was her.

She'd been dressed in black leather with cutouts appropriate for the scene intended, draped with chains and bent into a bondage device with that lovely head between her knees, a small rubber ball shoved into her mouth.

A bit ruffled, a few new bruises here and there, but that same blazing determination in the eyes and apparently none too worse for the indignities suffered.

Bolan ejected the ball from her mouth and tenderly removed her from the contraption, then sat on the floor and cuddled her in his arms. "It's okay," he murmured. "Hey, it's okay."

She was crying, sobbing freely with the emotional release of the moment. And it occurred to Bolan that she had not done that before. She settled down quickly, rubbing her face against his shoulder and clinging to him as she said, "I knew you'd come. I just kept saying hang on, babe, hang on. Your nice old giant will come. That lunatic, that creep. He makes porno movies down here. He tossed me in that gadget and made me watch a sample of his art. He does *snuff* films, Mack. I swear it is. It's too realistic for anything else." She shuddered. "He said I'm his newest star. Imagine that, little Suzie Landry, newest queen of snuff porn. That's a one-shot deal, isn't it?"

Bolan told her, "We have to move it. Can you find some clothes?"

She gestured vaguely toward a chair near the projector. "Where is *he*?" she whispered.

"Don't even ask," Bolan said. He knew the guy would turn up in some dark corner before the escapade was ended. Guys like Tony Morello quit trying only when they quit breathing. He found the clothing and helped her into it.

"They say the third time is a charm," she said huskily as he fastened the blouse over that heaving bosom.

"I found it that way the first time," he gruffly told her. Then he lifted her off her feet and carried her toward the exit of that abominable place.

"I heard the explosions," she said, the voice still a bit grainy. "And I thought, oh boy, here he comes. Loony-rello tossed that sheet over me and beat it, I guess. I could hear him running off. But then you didn't come and you didn't come. I was afraid you wouldn't know where to find me. And that damn ball stuck in my mouth—I could hardly breathe. I kept thinking, what if my nose stops up? Oh Mack, you should *see* that awful *film*! How could a human being *do* that to another? My God, you wouldn't *believe* . . ."

But he would. Bolan would believe.

It was the message he'd been trying to get across to her from the beginning.

But now he simply told her, "I'm glad I found you."

"Ohhh, so am I. Promise me, please, promise you'll never let me go again."

But he couldn't. He could not promise her that.

Someone was beating like crazy on the inside of a door on the main deck. Bolan set his lady on her feet, took the AutoMag in hand, and kicked that

151

door open. The two cute kids he'd noted earlier that day stumbled out of there, weeping and chattering hysterically in Italian.

It figured. These two were regulars—"starlets," probably—for the endless stream of 8mm porn pouring from Tony Morello's instant money machine. They were babies, barely into their teens if Bolan was any judge of womanflesh. And it seemed that Bad Tony was importing more than guns from Sicily.

Bolan managed to limp through some quick if mangled instructions in the Italian tongue. The kids understood it, anyway. They took off like a shot, and they knew which way to go.

Bolan followed, pulling his lady behind him, and he gave her also some quick instructions in the survival tongue. "When you get outside, head for the nearest railing. Do not wait for me and do not look back. Hit the water and swim like hell."

"What . . . about you?" she gasped.

"If I'm not right behind you then I won't be coming, babe."

"I'll wait for you!"

"Dammit, you'll do as I say!" He stepped through the hatch with the AutoMag up and ready, then pulled her out and shoved her off. "Hit it!" he hissed.

They'd exited from the main deck housing onto the ship's quarter. Two large cargo hatches took up most of the main deck from that point to the ship's stern where another small housing formed the fantail. Although the hatch covers extended several feet above the deck, it was a relatively clear area except for a winch station and some cargo handling booms between the hatches.

Above and behind Bolan, the entire superstructure was in flames. Off in the distance, a couple of small Coast Guard vessels were bearing hard on the disaster scene. Numerous other small boats were streaming out from the port area.

Bolan was moving one pace behind the girl, alert to any threat to their withdrawal. And they were about halfway home when that stern housing began spitting out hardmen—and they came out shooting. Bolan unleashed Big Thunder, sending out eight big splattering bullets that changed some minds back there and gave the girl time to reach the ship's rail. She paused there, though, crouching down and sending a stricken look back to the man with the thundering pistol. He had already ejected the spent clip and replaced it with a live one.

He yelled, "Go, dammit, *go!*"

"Not without you!" she cried.

And then Bolan spotted Bad Tony. Or, rather, Bad Tony spotted himself. In inimitable fashion. The maniac had risen from the protective cover of the after cargo hatch, Thompson submachine gun in hand, to spray his own cowering troops.

"*Malacarni* my ass!" he screamed. "You're a bunch of old women!"

It was an Old World term for the brave and the bold. And all these boys had wanted were some greener pastures. Bolan felt no particular sympathy. He simply saw it as another abomination in the unbelievable character of Bad Tony Morello. And yeah, Freddy—the guy had gone completely bananas.

Bolan raised the AutoMag and squeezed off a single round, the thundering report blending with and stilling the guttural staccato of the other insanely bucking weapon.

A huge red hole appeared in the area where Bad

153

Tony's rotten nose had once been, the heavy slug flattening on impact and splattering on through, ever growing in diameter and reaming an ever wider path through a brain which never had really functioned properly. The instrument of liberation exploded through the back side of that collapsing skull and kept on going, loath to be imprisoned there in such a foul environment.

Bad Tony died with his Thompson on.

And Mack Bolan was not "trying" those *malacarni*, those still alive, with any thoughts of gratitude. He grabbed his lady and dropped her overboard, then gladly quit that place himself.

But now, for sure, Bad Tony Morello had no more damn bananas.

19
FITTINGS

A fleet of small boats from the port had picked up all the survivors and several fireboats were working the fire problem. The Coast Guard was standing by and directing operations. Ben Logan was in working khakis and a Colt .45 was strapped to his side. A boarding party of whitehats with rifles and sidearms stood behind him. The captain knelt at the open gate of the cutter's railing talking in quiet tones to Mack Bolan who was in a small boat alongside.

"I'm not at all surprised to see you here, Sergeant," he said, eyes glinting warmly.

"Me either you," Bolan replied. He sponged water from his face with a borrowed towel as he added, "Good to see you in work uniform."

"Well ... I'd like you to know ... I was coming out after this bucket when I saw her blow. I, uh, worked out that problem with the lady. You were right. She's a hell of a fighter."

Bolan grinned tiredly and very enjoyably informed the man: "Bad Tony is no more. You'll find him on the fantail. I don't know where he keeps his goodies but if I were you I'd do a public service to some good citizens of Cleveland and shake that bucket down from stem to stern. Then I'd make a cozy bonfire with all the poison I found there. That's what I'd do."

Logan smiled. "Sounds like what any public-spirited citizen would do. Look. I can't say thanks. That simply isn't enough. If, uh, I were in your position, I think I'd like to know that the civil authorities ashore are combing the city and setting up roadblocks for a certain fugitive. And I, uh, would want to keep well clear of all primary roads."

Bolan said, "You're entirely welcome."

That good smile broadened. "Have you read John Donne?"

"No man is an island, right."

"No man is an entire continent either, Sergeant. He's just a piece of it. Try to remember that. And keep your head down."

Bolan grinned. "You, too. Don't go baring your breast to the commandant. Wear your own burdens. The world has too many saviours hanging from crosses already."

"I see you read Richard Harris also."

"Every chance I get, yes. Don't pass the judgment to others, Cap'n. Seriously. They'll tear you apart."

"You're a remarkable man. How did you *ever* get off into . . ." He changed his mind, deciding not to say that. "Keep on," he said.

Bolan smiled, glanced at his wet, woeful lady, and replied, "What else?"

"Of course I'm still alive," Bolan said to Leo Turrin. "What gave you the idea I wouldn't be?"

"I dunno, unless it could be that your four o'clock report came on like a last will and testament."

"Well . . . it's A-OK here for the moment. I may have a bit of trouble getting out of town. May decide to just, uh, cool it for a few days."

"You and the wild card, eh? Just thee and she and deception makes three."

Bolan's tone went suddenly very solemn as he responded to that. "Okay. I've been waiting for it. Give it. First—did Hal see my file?"

"He saw it, yes. Where's the babe? She there with you now?"

"Zonked out on the bed, yeah. Whatever else she may be, Leo, right now she is at the end of human endurance. The kid has been through a lot of hell since this time last night. More than a lot of hard men I know could take as well. I'm telling you right off the top of the cut that my instincts all go with her. Now. Overturn it."

The little guy sighed. "I don't know what she is, Sarge. That's for you to say. But I know what her grandfather is."

"You know for sure."

"Not the kind of sure we'd want to take into court, no. The kind of sure that your gut knows is right, yeah. He is your fateat, buddy. And I'll bet I can give you the names of his co-conspirators. There's a Eugene Scofflan, Cleveland Cooperative Consumers Inc. And a Michael D. O'Shea, chairman of Lake Trade Enterprises, that's a conglomerate, director status with a dozen others. Then you've got Aubrey Hirschbaum. If I have to give you his pedigree then you haven't been reading Fortune magazine or the Wall Street Journal much."

"Hirschbaum's in this?"

"Clear up to his neck. Hal has a dozen old phone taps linking him directly to the western syndicate—that is, the Jewish interests—and a couple from six months ago indicating a very chummy relationship with your good buddy Tony Morello."

"Uh-huh. Morello's dead, by the way."

"By the way, huh?"

"Yeah. So how is Paceman tied with these guys?"

"Scofflan has been his chief sponsor for years, chief fund raiser, and booster. Conversely, Scofflan's personal fortune has not been hurt a damn bit by the friendship. He has had a, uh, uncanny sense of timing ever since Paceman became a power on various committees. You know—buying and selling at just the right time to insure a killing."

"And O'Shea?"

"A new boy in town. Came there from Detroit two years ago. Brought his corporate headquarters with him. Just in time to benefit from legislative largesse. He and Scofflan now share ownership in a fancy yacht on which the Honorable Mister Paceman also takes frequent cruises. The four wives are closest pals."

"Where does Hirschbaum fit in there?"

"He's just the guy that put Paceman in office the first time. That was back in the days when the Jewish gangs practically owned Ohio. Hirschbaum, it turns out, owned Franklin Adams Paceman. He's owned him ever since."

Bolan sighed heavily. "Why is all this just now coming out, Leo?"

"What the hell, guy, it's your game. Nobody knows better than you. It's a matter of punching the right buttons at the right time. I'm sorry if you don't like the can of worms—but it's your can, pal, and you're the guy that opened it."

"You mean it's gas connected."

"You got it. Paceman has the fatcat role. Between the other three and all their devious interconnections, they have a damn hefty stranglehold on *all* the industrial energy supplies for not only Ohio but for the whole damn northeast. Add in some of the names on your pigeon list and it's an absolute power monopoly."

"So what's the feeling in Wonderland, Leo? What will they do with it?"

"The feeling is that they will probably first withhold supplies. They'll shut down industries in wholesale lots from Michigan to Maine, and they—"

"All right, but give me an argument. How could they do that?"

"They simply do it. They claim shortage, nonavailability, whatever they damn well please. Have you taken a look at the federal energy programs lately? No? I'll tell you why. There isn't one. Nobody knows what the true energy situation is in this country. Those guys can cap their wells and shut down the transmission pipes and simply say, well, fellas, we're out of gas. Too bad about that. And there's *no*body to say different."

Bolan said, "Okay, that's about the way I see it. Thanks for the argument. I guess there's no argument whatever about step two."

"Cut and dried, I guess, yeah. They'll jump the price about a zillion percent. They'll bankrupt companies far and wide, then gobble them up. They'll absolutely control the economy of the entire nation and—by logical extension—of goodly parts of the free world. Only it won't be so free anymore."

Bolan said, "Could they really do it?"

"The feeling is, yeah, they could do it. Especially if we get a hard winter. That's the only fingerhold they'd need. That would be the government's breakpoint. We just don't have the machinery to deal with it on a hurry-hurry basis. It could take years of courtroom maneuvering. By then, well, let's just pray for warm winters."

"These guys aren't Mafia, Leo."

"Fellow travelers, though. Hirschbaum is as mean as any. He just doesn't carry a gun."

"Morello carried the guns for them."

"Right. That's the way it works."

Bolan said, "Okay. Let's get some murder indictments on Paceman, Scofflan, O'Shea, and Hirschbaum. The employer is as guilty as the employee. Right?"

Turrin laughed. "You're developing a very weird sense of humor."

Bolan chuckled with him. "Yeah. Okay. So we'll buck it up to a higher court."

"You got one of those?"

"Yeah. It just found them guilty."

"You the judge?"

"No. I'm the judgment."

"Good luck, pal. Step lightly."

Bolan hung up and turned troubled eyes toward the bedroom. Step lightly, yeah, sure. So where did *she* fit?

160

20
CONNED

Those great luminous blues flashed up at him and she purred contentedly. "Ohhhh great, I dreamed you were gone and I was trying to catch you in my sailboat. But you just strode on with those ten-league strides, straight out across Erie. I'm glad. I mean that it was a dream."

He gently inquired, "You okay?"

"I'm fine now, yes, thank you." She patted the bed invitingly. "Don't you ever rest?"

He told her, "I can't rest yet, Susan. We need to parley. We need to square it up."

Those eyes closed for a moment. A small tear popped loose and rolled along the velvety course. "Okay," she said, after a moment. "Let's square it up."

"That Pine Grove list—I know—"

She bit it. "Sorry, that's still confidential."

He said, "I wasn't asking you. I was about to tell

you. I know where you got it. It came from your grandfather, Senator Paceman."

Those eyes flared wide. "Why don't you just let it *go*?" she moaned.

"I can't let it go. You conned me. Now we have to square the con or there's nothing possible between us, nothing at all. I'll put on my ten-league boots and I'll say goodbye."

"Oh wow, you're such a granite block of solid morality, aren't you? So square, so perfect, such a fine masculine example for all your kids to follow. Ha!"

He said, "There won't be any kids. And I am what I am. Goodbye, Susan."

He was at the door when she yelled, "Well, wait a minute, dammit! Okay! Okay! I conned you! Does that square it?"

He turned to her with a pained smile. "It's a beginning."

"Look I—I'm *not* going to hand over any heads for you."

"You mean, you're not going to hand over your grandfather's head. That's been the problem all along, hasn't it? All of your squawling and posturing about justice and legal rights . . . you've just been trying to cover for that dirty old man."

She looked as though he'd slapped her. Those eyes recoiled and lashed back at him, then quickly subsided and fell to an inspection of her own hands. "Okay," she said, small voiced. "Maybe I deserve that. And maybe *he* deserves it. But I'm not going to let you put a bullet in him."

"What makes you so sure I want to? I didn't put one in Logan. Or in Sorenson. The only people so honored were Morello and his crazies. I just want it all out front between you and me. I want it squared."

Very quietly she said, "I worked for him from time to time. School vacations. Elections. Various little things. He was more than a grandpa. All my life he was a second father. Last of a line." Another tear popped out. "The last of the Pacemans. My mother was his only child. And he always felt very bad about that. The family tree was withering up."

"You were working for him," Bolan prodded.

"Oh, just casual little tasks. But still every time I go to Grandpa's I go into his study and sort of tidy up—you know, catch up his filing, empty his cigar butts, you know."

Bolan sighed. "And you're a curious kid."

She took it with a half smile. "Guess I always was. I can remember his scolding me when I was ten years old, for going through his desk. Well ... six weeks ago I was doing the same thing. That's when I found the list. I was ... shocked. Stunned is the word. Because, you see, here's the irony. I really *was* thinking of doing a story on the society deaths. And it blew me out to find those names on the list. I, uh, I just had to check it out."

"But you didn't begin the check at Grandpa's lap, eh?"

"Of course not. Franklin Adams Paceman simply is not a man to be confronted with vile and hasty suspicions." She peered up at him from behind another half smile. "No bullets? Truly?"

He smiled back. "That would hardly be a way to cement our relationship, would it? But this is very interesting. Go on."

"Well ... dammit ... call a spade by its name, Susan. I have known ... for some time ... that

Grandpa was . . ." She held a hand flatly extended and wiggled it. "I mean . . ."

"Kinky, I think, is the word," Bolan said wryly.

"Well, I was going for something not quite so harsh. Politically expedient, let's say. He did a lot of wheeling and dealing. But he used to say that politics was a game of chance. And you had to make your own chances, if you meant to be an effective instrument of government."

"But you found some extracurricular instruments, eh?"

"Oh, nothing to really put a finger on. It was just a . . . a feeling. You know, an atmosphere."

Yeah. Bolan knew those atmospheres quite well.

"And I was a bit disturbed by some of his friends."

"Guys like Hirschbaum," he said.

Those eyes recoiled again. "Who's been conning *whom*?" she flared.

"But Grandpa didn't send you to the country club, eh?"

"Of course not!" The gaze wavered and finally broke. "I told you I was on a story. It's true. I was. But I soon discovered . . . it was a story that could never be written."

"So why did you stay with it?"

"I hoped to . . . get enough facts . . . with which . . . to confront . . ."

"You were going for a coverup. You just wanted to safe the family. At any cost."

"That's unfair! My God he's my grandfather! He used to bounce me on his knee and tell me fairytales! What was I supposed to do? I was going to write my story, okay, *yes*! But for his eyes only! I wanted him to *know* that *I* knew!"

"You were going to club him with it."

"Yes, to put it bluntly, exactly that. He was going to retire from politics."

"And put all the loot back?"

She said, "Let's be reasonable."

"That's what *he* would say."

"I—I guess so."

"Susan, you are shamefully naive. That old man would put you on a spit and roast you. Retire from politics? Nothing but a bullet can retire that guy now. He's owned body and soul by a syndicate powerful enough to put a man in the White House. You think they'd let him retire? Or that *he* would even consent to it? You're—"

"You said *no* bullets!"

"That's what I said, right. But I want you to *understand* what you really know. Do you believe for a moment that Morello caught you with your hands in the goodie box and kept the secret from his associates? You think he didn't have you going in—from the moment you first stumbled? You think Grandpa *did not know* that Morello had his hands on you?"

She was bawling again. And that was good. Yeah, that was very good.

She was under control again, sipping hot chocolate and watching him with reddened eyes. He told her, "I'm sorry I had to drag you through that. But you had to face it. And the sooner the better. Those guys had to make a command decision. You had blown their little game with Judge Daly. He was a vital link in their chain of power. Morello wasn't the brains of the game. He was just the muscle. And they had the guy under fantastic pressure. Loony-rello, as you called him, was not accustomed to parlor games of power intrigue. He's a very direct savage—hit 'em and run, that's his *modus*. His first instinct must have been to sandbag you damn quick. I'm not saying that the Big Four knew about that first try. But they *had* to know about the follow-up. Morello *had* to tell them because it was his only excuse for failure."

"Yes I—I see that," she weepily admitted. "And I—I think, now that it's opened up, I—I think Grandpa or his friends must have been contacted even before they took me to the pool. They were holding me in the pro shop. And there were a number of telephone conversations. Very urgent conversations. Oh, three or four."

"And they didn't try to sweat you for information."

"No. How'd you know?"

He gave her a knowing look. "Just by looking at you, twit."

"I'm not a twit."

Bolan grinned. "What is a twit?"

"I'm not sure. Sort of a shrew, isn't it? Anyway, I'm not one."

"I made it up," he admitted, grinning. "Took a verb and made it a noun. Like *truce*."

She colored and told him, "We could try that on again, you know."

"No reason why not," he said. "We're all square now, aren't we?"

"Not quite."

"Well—let's tuck it all in, girl."

"The second time Morello snatched me . . . I had just come from an office in the Terminal Tower. Your reasoning is perfect. The office is leased by Mr. Hirschbaum."

"Uh-huh. Still trying to beard the lion, huh? After all my warnings."

"Yes, well, as you said ... I'm terribly naive, I guess. I had to make one last try. I couldn't even get past the reception desk. They kept me waiting for about ten minutes, then turned me out. Morello's goons were waiting for me outside."

Bolan released a long, weary sigh.

"So they knew Morello had me that time, for sure. They sicced him on me. And there was a final contact. You remember? I called your mobile number and we had to wait while you called back? Morello called *them* during that period. I knew it was them by the way Morello kowtowed. He told them that he had your h-head in his pocket. And he was laughing as he told them how he'd put it there. There was a lot of joviality. They wanted him to come to this meeting and he was trying to get out of it, trying to assure them that everything was okay now. He mentioned Judge Daly several times. You must have that call on your collectors."

"Those collectors are no more," he told her. "And I collected nothing after that first call from you."

"Oh. Well. Anyway, Morello convinced them that everything was okay now. They talked some about Judge Daly and his probable replacement in the scheme. And he did not want to attend that meeting. Told them he'd been up all night and all day. He was tired and besides his ship was wounded. He was sending it somewhere for repairs—some drydock which he referred to as a 'snug harbor.' And he wanted to go along and take that chance to unwind and rest up. And he looked at me and laughed as he was telling them that. There was a lot of snickering and I knew that *I* was the subject of that. But Grandpa could not possibly have known what that lunatic had in mind for me. He could *not.*"

Bolan replied, "Probably not, no. Grandpa himself maybe didn't know about any of that. Let's think it that way, eh?"

"Yes, God yes, there's no other way to think it."

Very casually he asked her, "Where was that meeting?"

She shook her head. "I didn't catch that. It was for ten o'clock."

"Tonight?"

"Uh-huh."

He glanced at his watch. "Guess I should take that in, then."

Those eyes withdrew again. She gasped, "You said—you promised . . ."

"Relax," he said. "I'm just playing your game now. You said the Terminal Tower?"

"Well, I don't know where they're meeting! You promised me, Mack. Damn you, you *promised!*"

He sighed and said, "Your game, Susan. Your way."

"You'll just 'club' him?"

"I'm not the judge, Susan. I'll let him be his own."

She sighed and relaxed, taking that explanation favorably.

"I'd best get going. It's already past ten. Go back to sleep. Wake you when I get back." He smiled sadly. "We'll truce a bit when all the hurts are better."

She said, very quietly, "No truce is possible, Mack, with blood between us. Understand that."

He understood that.

"See you later," he said, and went out of there.

Bolan took a cab to the yacht club at Edgewater Park and reclaimed his battle cruiser. It was more than that, of course. It was also base camp, mission control, home. All tamper seals were intact, indicating no breach of cover security.

He changed into a quiet business suit and rummaged through a file of ID wallets until he found one he liked. The Beretta Belle was snugged beneath the suit jacket at the left arm.

The time was nearly ten-thirty when he fired the power plant and sent the big cruiser back onto the streets of Cleveland.

Police patrols were in great evidence. The radio scanners were showing plenty of activity on the official airwaves, also. The downtown streets were relatively calm and quiet, though. He nosed the cruiser into a commercial park-yourself lot and went the rest of the way on foot.

It was a nice night, very clear, stars twinkling from their faraway habitats. And Bolan felt about that far, at the moment, from . . .

Right, Susan. Bloodied truces were a bit difficult to manage.

He signed in at the security station in the lobby, showing the uniformed guard federal credentials and telling him, "No announcements. I get up there and discover I was expected, I'll come down all over your ass with enough charges to bury you forever."

The guy went white and assured the federal agent that no announcements would be forthcoming.

He took the elevator to the thirty-fifth floor and found the suite of offices he sought behind gilt-edged lettering:

CLEVELAND PIPELINE ASSOCIATES

How appropriate.

The reception room was brightly lighted. A guy in wrinkled plaids sprawled there with a *Playboy* at his lap.

Bolan asked him, "Are they here?"

The guy asked, "Who are you?"

Bolan showed him the credentials with the left hand and chopped him with the right as the guy bent toward the inspection. He fell back into the chair with a grunt. An ID wallet revealed the role. He was a Pinkerton.

Sure. Very clean, very proper.

Bolan found The Four in a large central office made up like a board room. Gleaming mahogany panels at the walls, highly polished circular table with cush chairs of crushed velour, the ever necessary portable bar with all the juices, four very startled "gentlemen" gaping disapprovingly at the intrusion.

Though he'd never placed eyes there before, Bolan could identify each of these "gentlemen" in his own place.

There was the silver-haired and sleekly sophisticated politician who'd built a lifetime on the take and erected a Hollywood shell around that rotten core. Paceman.

And the boyish executive with eyes that could snap from puckish to malicious with the twitch of a lid, a real live Neanderthal with twentieth century manners and a cannibal's appetite. O'Shea.

Slot Two held the shyster lawyer *cum* instant millionnaire, a shifty-eyed scoundrel who'd sell you a car with no engine but guarantee full satisfaction on all nonmechanical parts in the small print. Scofflan.

Finally, *Numero Uno*—hearty chairman of a

dozen nonexistent corporations with fat accounts in too many foreign banks to count, not a Jew but a *kike*, the kind who gives a fine race that terrible reputation, a guy whose only God is money and whose only morality lies in the fastest way to make it. Hirschbaum, sure.

The chairman of the board harrumphed and gnashed the stump of a cigar as he demanded an explanation for the uninvited visit. The others sat tensely with frosted drinks numbing the hands and tumbling thoughts, no doubt, enervating the brains.

Bolan dropped a marksman's medal to the shiny table.

"Susan sends it with love," he said coldly.

Paceman twitched, and those eyes revealed the horribly nasty truth.

O'Shea and Scofflan simply looked stunned.

The chairman tried to turn it around. "Thank God she's all right," he boomed heartily. "You must be the young man who's responsible for all the ruckus around town today. Can't really say I approve but ..." He laughed heartily and shook his head while regarding the "young man" with a warmly tolerant face. "You do get results, don't you?"

Bolan replied, "Usually." He brought the Belle up and sent nine millimeters worth of results sighing into that warmly tolerant but quickly collapsing face.

O'Shea flung his arms backward in pure reflex, eyes twitching rapidly from malicious to puckish to pure boyish terrified. Round two added a third eye, pure mortal dead.

Scofflan made a run for it while the politician hung in there grimly for the final vote tally. Neither found comfort from rounds three and four.

A blue folder fat with legalistic papers sat face up between the chairman's dead hands. It was labeled CLEVELAND PIPELINE. Bolan retrieved the death medal and dropped it atop the bloodied folder.

And, yes, how very appropriate.

He ran into a highly distraught young lady on the sidewalk just outside the Terminal Tower, and he said, "Shame on you, Susan. You didn't trust me."

Hope flickered there as she tried to respond to that. "I—I remembered ... you told me a safe house is safe but once. I was afraid you weren't coming back. I—I *knew* ..."

He said, "It's okay now."

"Was he there? Did you talk to him?"

Bolan nodded. "He found himself guilty, Susan."

"Don't double-talk me, damn you!"

"You're right. Believe me, I am sorry. I gave him a bullet."

"*Damn* you! You *promised*!"

"I said your game, your way. You conned me, kid. I conned you back. None of it is on your hands. I'll wear it. Without shame. He earned it. Believe it."

"It wasn't for *him*, dammit! It was for *them*! My mother and my grandmother! How could you make me *do* that to them?"

"You didn't do it to them," Bolan said wearily. "In truth, neither did I. *He* did it to them. Long time ago. All those years, masquerading as a man. All the while, nothing but a shell with maggots inside."

She cried, "Oh, *God*!"

He said, sadly, "It's goodbye, I guess."

172

Those blues flashed, then quickly receded. "Yes. I guess it is."

He started to walk away.

"Mack! I *am* going to write this story!"

"Good for you. Watch the quotes."

She smiled feebly. "Nice old giant. Nice old weary, miserable giant. Watch those ten-league boots, huh?"

He smiled back, trying to pack an eternity into one final look—then he went on and did not look back.

No man was an island, no—nor an entire continent. At the moment, this one felt not even like a piece of one.

It was the ultimate con job, perhaps. Upon himself, by himself.

All he knew was that he was headed for the loneliest "home" in the universe.

But at least, by God, it would not be the coldest. The Cleveland pipes would flow next winter.

He hoped.

Epilogue

Dateline Cleveland. Slug it: "Baby, It's Gonna Get Cold Outside"

This began as a story I could never write. Well, tonight I'm writing it. Tomorrow I hope the whole world will be reading it. It's a story not so much of greed and unbridled lust and rotten people as it is a story of human gallantry, unbelievable personal sacrifice, the sublimation of an entire magnificent human personality into the grim necessities of maintaining our precious civilization by whatever tools are handy, by whatever means can point toward a positive good.

It's a savage world, the man said, and the meek shall never inherit while the savages rule the heights. The man who said that is Mack Bolan, a tremendous giant who strolls all the heights and who *could* rule, you better believe it, but chooses instead to serve the meek.

I am in love with this man. I so proclaim it to all the world and one day I hope to lie in his arms again as I did so unreservedly and so very proudly earlier today. But let this revelation not cloud the story I am about to tell—because, as you shall see, there are two sides to every human relationship— and this man also coldly and with great premeditation executed my own grandfather a few short hours ago.

"I gave him a bullet," said Mack the Giant as though he had conferred some sort of honor thereby.

And maybe he did. I will tell the story and let the reader judge. It began one chilling day in the study of my grandfather's home. His name is, or was, Franklin Adams Paceman—a proud name, is it not? No, it is not. You see, my grandfather was a rotten shell of a man with nothing but maggots inside. I know this may sound . . .

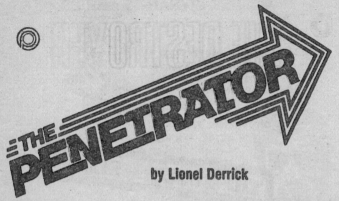

THE PENETRATOR

by Lionel Derrick

Mark Hardin. Discharged from the army, after service in Vietnam. His military career was over. But *his* war was just beginning. His reason for living and reason for dying become the same—to stamp out crime and corruption wherever he finds it. He is deadly; he is unpredictable; and he is dedicated. He is The Penetrator!

Read all of him in:

Order		Title	Book No.	Price
_____	# 1	THE TARGET IS H	P236	$ .95
_____	# 2	BLOOD ON THE STRIP	P237	$ .95
_____	# 3	CAPITOL HELL	P318	$ .95
_____	# 4	HIJACKING MANHATTAN	P338	$ 95
_____	# 5	MARDI GRAS MASSACRE	P378	$ .95
_____	# 6	TOKYO PURPLE	P434	$1.25
_____	# 7	BAJA BANDIDOS	P502	$1.25
_____	# 8	THE NORTHWEST CONTRACT	P540	$1.25
_____	# 9	DODGE CITY BOMBERS	P627	$1.25
_____	#10	THE HELLBOMB FLIGHT	P690	$1.25

TO ORDER

Please check the space next to the book/s you want, send this order form together with your check or money order, include the price of the book/s and 25¢ for handling and mailing, to:

PINNACLE BOOKS, INC. / P.O. Box 4347
Grand Central Station / New York, N. Y. 10017

☐ Check here if you want a free catalog.

I have enclosed $_____ check_____ or money order_____ as payment in full. No C.O.D.'s.

Name_____

Address_____

City_____ State_____ Zip_____
(Please allow time for delivery)

PB-40

THE "BUTCHER,"
the only man to leave
the Mafia—and live!
A man forever on the run,
unable to trust anyone,
condemned to a life
of constant violence!

THE BUTCHER SERIES

Order		Title	Book #	Price
_____	# 1	KILL QUICK OR DIE	P011	.95
_____	# 2	COME WATCH HIM DIE	P025	.95
_____	# 3	KEEPERS OF DEATH	P603	1.25
_____	# 4	BLOOD DEBT	P111	.95
_____	# 5	DEADLY DEAL	P152	.95
_____	# 6	KILL TIME	P197	.95
_____	# 7	DEATH RACE	P228	.95
_____	# 8	FIRE BOMB	P608	1.25
_____	# 9	SEALED WITH BLOOD	P279	.95
_____	#10	THE DEADLY DOCTOR	P291	.95
_____	#11	VALLEY OF DEATH	P332	.95
_____	#12	KILLER'S CARGO	P429	1.25
_____	#13	BLOOD VENGEANCE	P539	1.25
_____	#14	AFRICAN CONTRACT	P583	1.25
_____	#15	KILL GENTLY, BUT SURE	P671	1.25
_____	#16	SUICIDE IN SAN JUAN	P726	1.25
_____	#17	THE CUBANO CAPER	P794	1.25
_____	#18	THE U.N. AFFAIR	P843	1.25
_____	#19	MAYDAY OVER MANHATTAN	P869	1.25
_____	#20	THE HOLLYWOOD ASSASSIN	P893	1.25

TO ORDER
Please check the space next to the book/s you want, send this order form
together with your check or money order, include the price of the book/s
and 25¢ for handling and mailing to:
PINNACLE BOOKS, INC. / P.O. BOX 4347
Grand Central Station / New York, N.Y. 10017

☐ CHECK HERE IF YOU WANT A FREE CATALOG

I have enclosed $_____ check _____ or money order _____ as
payment in full. No C.O.D.'s.

Name_____

Address_____

City_____ State_____ Zip_____
(Please allow time for delivery.)   PB-37